THE CUBAN MANUSCRIPT

LILIAN GEORGE

The Cuban Manuscript
A novel by Lilian George

Published by Lilian George Books

This is a work of fiction. Names, characters, places, and incidents are either the product of the author's imagination or are used fictitiously. Any resemblance to actual persons, living or dead, events, or locales is entirely coincidental.

ISBN-13 (paperback): 979-8-9942204-0-5
ISBN-13 (ebook): 979-8-9942204-1-2

To my daughter, whose light outshines
all else in my life.

CONTENTS

A NOTE FROM THE AUTHOR

Those pages carry every beat of dread, every taste of hunger, every whispered prayer in the dark millions endured under the communist regimes that promised paradise and delivered only chains.

I write for America's youth—passionate, tech-savvy, often blind to history's scars. Socialism isn't "social justice"; it is control disguised as compassion, seizing thought, speech, and production. With today's technology, that control would be absolute, irreversible. Liberty is fragile—one heartbeat from loss.

In 2020, I self-published a warning; algorithms buried it, branding a child stepping on the Soviet hammer and sickle as "violent." Five turbulent years later—pandemic, unrest, and silenced voices—*The Cuban Manuscript* rises, the Cuban chapter now woven into the warning. PTSD haunted the writing, but the cost is nothing compared to the goal: awaken one mind before the cage closes.

To the friends who urged me past fear, my editor's patience with accent-tinted drafts, the designer who captured the soul—thank you. To my late parents, who taught me to treasure freedom; to my daughter, my fiercest critic, whose fair heart sparks our debates; to the man who risked everything to guide me across the Iron Curtain —your light endures.

America remains the world's hope. Unity demands common ground. Learn from history. Choose light.

November 2025

SPUDS AND SHACKLES

The apartment was a creaky cage, cramming Liana, her parents, and three aunts into walls so thin that the wind mocked them, snow dusting their dreams like a cruel jest, streaming through gaps in the old, crooked window frames. The wooden floor sounded like a dysfunctional orchestra, rising to an impossible crescendo near the entry door, announcing every move of its patrons with haunting screeching. Inside, it was clean and neat, but poverty screamed from every angle. Nostalgia seeped from the once-beautiful armchairs, their springs protruding through painfully thinning leather, wrinkled and cracked, exhausted from years of use. Liana had to carefully choose where to sit, or she might get pinched by the metal—not a pleasant experience, after all. A dinner table stood firm, its polished wood bearing a quality unseen amid decades of decay in the world outside.

It was a desperate, dangerous time. The Soviet regime in her East European country played the vicious mother-in-law, its rules a whip cracking over people's lives, promising a socialist paradise where potatoes were breakfast, lunch, and ambition. At twelve, Liana teetered between a child's wonder and a teenager's scowl, her belly growling louder than the radio's hymns to the Party. Why did some feast while she counted spuds? Some people had it all—their homes were big, their phones were approved without years of waiting, and their refrigerators were filled with food. Her parents didn't even have a fridge; after all, if they had one, it would have stayed empty anyway. Those people were special, faithful guardians of communist ideology; their children didn't wait for their parents' paydays to savor a scrap of meat—a festival in Liana's gray world, where most nights brought cabbage or rice, when stores managed to stock it. Her cat, Miska, a wiry survivor, lived on crumbs, a diet that'd make modern vets clutch their pearls in horror. The cat died from illness, with no vet to help in Liana's barren world, and she cried helplessly, refusing to let her parents take the stiffened, cold body of her little friend from her hands. They were all heroes, she thought wryly, forced to grow up too soon by a regime that peddled utopia but delivered only empty plates and tears in abundance.

Obedience was the golden rule, pressed into the entire nation's terrified minds and passed to Liana like a lead weight. Late-night knocks—sharp as a commissar's boots on gravel—froze them at their scarred table, plates licked clean like starved dogs. Her father's face drained whiter than the snow piling outside, his eyes locking with her mother's in a silent pact. "To the room," he'd rasp, voice splintered. In the bedroom they shared, Liana's bony chest tightened, sweat soaking her as she prayed—a crime, her schoolteacher barked daily; never pray, never hold religion, or you'd doom your future, your family's future, and those to come. Still, Liana prayed, unsure who she was praying to, envisioning God as an old, all-forgiving man sitting on a chair, with her hugging his shoulders, her eyes full of tears and hopes. She knew her father would vanish with those men in grim coats, sometimes for weeks, returning with eyes hollowed, and his voice a whisper she strained to hear. Her mother grew quieter, urging Liana to comply, a bitter pill for her stubborn streak, but she obliged—for them.

Her father's sin was unforgivable: he was born to a family that served the old government, now crushed by the glorious Soviet Army—those Russian-boot-wearing soldiers were heroes, the radio crowed, liberating them into misery. His uncle, a proud official, faced a firing squad after a farce of a trial, his portrait stuffed in a drawer among moth-eaten clothes. The regime tried to "fix" her father with electric shocks in an internment camp, his scars a secret Liana learned about years later, after his death, when her mother's trembling voice spilled the truth over a chipped teacup. Her aunts were banished to distant villages across the country, the Party's cure for rebel thoughts, their letters arriving like ghosts—thin and weary. From an early age, Liana learned to play the marionette, her lips moving to the Party's tune while her heart screamed "no." That defiance, born in hunger and fear, burned brighter with every new day. She sang the Party's tunes at school, while praying quietly in her heart, and that tiny voice was stronger than any hymn, despite the fear of far-reaching consequences. It was triggered by that remarkable resilience in her father's eyes, which he tried to hide, worried that his daughter was much like him—a wild horse refusing to let anyone triumph over her freedom.

Back then, in Eastern Europe, Liana didn't fully understand what was happening around her. She knew about the Iron Curtain —her mind tried to picture what a curtain would look like … Was it really surrounding the entire country? Was it made of iron because it was supposed to be impenetrable? She knew some people were able to travel to and from Europe and the United States. How were they able to do it? As Liana matured, she realized that the curtain symbolized the division between liberty and oppression, and the world she lived in was consciously designed to deny her fellow compatriots their fundamental human rights, instead keeping them hungry, scared, controlled, powerless, and misinformed.

She couldn't see the future—she was still a child. All she could do was dream of that free world she'd heard existed, so desperately distant yet so passionately needed, not just for her, but for her parents, her aunts, and the school kids with hungry eyes, begging not only for food but for a sign of hope—perhaps illusory, but vivid —a fire burning bright, day after day, night after night, despite the desperation they lived in.

The regime had to find a way to lure the younger generations into embracing its failed ideas. The only tools it had were the negation of the successes beyond the Iron Curtain, relentless indoctrination, brainwashing, and propaganda. Summers, too, were a golden chance to harness the free labor of adolescents, keeping them too busy to ponder the grim reality surrounding them. And didn't they work for free! Countless Sundays and summers were swallowed by forced labor. Sometimes they swept streets or cleared roads, dust stinging their eyes; other times, they hauled bricks for construction, their small hands blistering and aching. One summer, Liana would never forget—she was twelve or thirteen. They were shipped to a remote village to toil in an agricultural cooperative for a month. They told her it grew fruits and vegetables, made pickles —a noble task for the collective good.

"It'll be a fun summer for all of you!" her school principal chirped, ordering the parents to pack them off. Liana's parents loathed it—her mom's eyes brimming with tears as she folded her clothes—but they had no say. No parent could shield their child from being exploited as free labor; defiance wasn't an option under the regime's iron fist.

School principals wielded power like policemen then, stationed at the entrance each morning, their eyes sharp as bayonets, scrutinizing uniforms for a loose thread, a missing red scarf, and sniffing out "anomalies" in behavior with the zeal of Party enforcers. They'd dole out punishments for "course correction"—no mere slap on the wrist or a call to parents, but a gauntlet of shame and fear designed to crush rebellion before it took root. Liana despised her school principal, a man with a face carved from stone, his voice a low growl that echoed the regime's propaganda, his office a tribunal where futures were weighed and often broken. A wayward glance, a whisper of dissent, or a skirt hemmed too high could earn a public humiliation before the class, a letter to the Party branding a family as suspect, or worse—a summons to the local commissar, where questions cut deeper than any blade, threatening expulsion, labor camps, or a lifetime of surveillance trailing like a shadow. Liana had seen classmates vanish, their desks empty after a single misstep, their parents' faces gray with dread at the next mandatory public meeting. The principal's punishments were a whip, cracking to keep young souls in line, their dreams irrevocably chained to the state's iron will.

Once, he summoned her mom to warn of her daughter's "dangerously free spirit" and her "frivolous ponytail," which he sneered "dangled in a manner unfit for our society's moral values." Her mom said nothing when she came home, but Liana overheard her whispering to her dad that night, their voices low as she feigned sleep in their shared room. The next morning, her mom braided her hair tightly, her fingers gentle but firm, and asked her to ditch the ponytail at school. Liana couldn't bear to question her—just kissed her cheek and promised to obey.

That summer, reluctantly, her mom packed a small bag: clothes, her only pair of shoes, and two sandwiches for the road. Hugs and kisses followed, and for the first time, Liana would be away from home for a whole month. After a jolting bus ride, they reached the village and split into groups—boys to one building, girls to an old cattle house. The ground floor reeked, a swamp of filth left from long-gone cows. The smell clawed at her throat. They climbed to the second floor, and Liana froze—vast and barren, not a chair, table, or bed in sight. Straw littered the floor like a mockery of comfort. Their teacher announced that they'd sleep on it. Thirty girls, thirty dark wool blankets tossed down on the floor—no sheets, no pillows. A lone bulb dangled from the ceiling, its sickly light barely cutting the gloom. The air was stifling; flies and mosquitoes swarmed, their buzz a relentless drone against the skin.

Outside, two squat toilets stood, crude and stinking, beside a lone shower—a rusted pipe bent at the top. "Keep your mouths closed," the teacher warned, "the water's contaminated." A rusty can of detergent sat under a shed for washing hands. But they were young, and nothing could fully dim their spirits! They dropped their bags and raced downstairs to the bus, bound for the eatery. The boys joined them, and soon they were laughing and chattering over simple yet warm food. After dinner, they formed a big circle under the vast sky, city lights a distant memory. The teachers lit a fire, its crackle magical as stars winked downward, whispering futures of hope to them—poor kids with unasked-for fates.

They kept them busy, making them rise one by one to praise the government, sing odes to the Soviet Union, Lenin, socialism, and their leaders—voices frail against the night. Exhausted from the day, they dozed off as darkness fell. No bus returned; a teacher led them back on foot. The village had few streetlights, but slivers of glow peeked from behind distant window curtains, guiding them to the farm. The farmhouse loomed dark, its single bulb casting a faint glow over their straw beds. Flies buzzed, the stench thickened, and the blankets scratched like burlap. Liana thought of home—the worn furniture, creaky floors, warped windows letting in rain and snow—and ached for its familiar embrace.

"One month! How will I survive without Mom and Dad?" Tears welled, loneliness swallowing her. The girl beside her whispered, "I miss my parents and grandparents." She reached out; they clasped hands, sobbing until sleep took them. Hours later, a clatter jolted her awake—girls screamed. A ladder hit the open window, and four or five men leaped in, burly, drunk, and aggressive. Cursing and laughing, they hollered, "Are there any p … to f …?" their flashlights raking over them. The teacher shrieked, shoving one of them, but they hurled her into a corner. "Run, girls, run!" she cried, her voice ragged, and they stumbled downstairs—dark steps, tripping, falling, rising, and trembling in terror. Outside, sobbing, she called their names, counting to ensure they were safe. Then came a piercing scream from above, then another, and a third—then silence. Liana's heart iced over.

The teacher bolted back inside. Villagers—men from nearby homes—rushed in too. Shouts erupted, a scuffle, and then a man emerged, cradling a girl from their group. Women with flashlights drew near, and they saw her—hair spilling back, face deathly pale, shirt torn, and blood streaking her bare legs. She was unconscious. "Go upstairs, girls!" the teacher sobbed. "It's safe now—they fled." "What happened?" the girls pleaded, their voices trembling with fear. "Her period came. We'll find a car for the hospital. Go upstairs—villagers will stay." Silently, they climbed back, lying on the straw. The prickling, the rough blankets, and the mosquito bites faded—they were numb, haunted by the sense that something unspeakable had struck. That dread lingered still; Liana relived every second of that night. Later, as she matured, she knew: it wasn't the girl's period. Those men raped her. Liana remembers her on the bus—her pretty face, long hair, and bright smile—and prays for her, unsure if she has survived. No phones, a few cars—who knows if help came in time to stop her bleeding, to save her for the long healing ahead?

They lay there, crying—terrified. They were just kids, cast out against their parents' will. Alone, her home a distant speck, Liana realized for the first time that someone far more powerful and monstrous endangered them—not just the school or principal, but a force vast and vile. Even if they screamed, no one would hear; they were defenseless. The next morning, they weren't chatty. They trudged to the eatery in silence, heads down, the night's terror still clinging to them like damp straw. Breakfast was a blur—thin porridge that stuck in their throats—then they marched to work. The cooperative workers, faces hard and indifferent, thrust dull knives into their hands and pointed to a mountain of onions, piled high in a corner of the barn. "Cut them, then jar them," they barked, handing them crystal jars that glinted mockingly in the dim light. They sat on rickety stools, the air thick with the sharp, stinging reek of onions, and began.

The first slices bit back—juice sprayed all over, stinging their eyes until tears streamed unchecked, blurring the blades. By day's end, their faces swelled, eyes burned red and raw, and their hands bore dozens of cuts, blood mixing with onion sting. Liana stared at her fingers, trembling, the skin splitting where the knife slipped—a pain so sharp it stole her breath. Day after day, week after week, they hacked at that endless heap. The pile shrank, then grew again as more sacks arrived, a cruel cycle with no end. Her hands turned into swollen, inflamed claws—each cut a throbbing wound, each onion a fresh assault. She'd flinch at the knives' glint, their edges dulled but still menacing. Dressing was torture; pulling a sleeve over her ravaged hands made her sob, the fabric snagging on open sores. The days dragged, each hour stretching longer than the last, a slow grind under the barn's stifling heat. The onion fumes choked her hope of a miracle early return home as flies buzzed around them, drawn to the mess, landing on their cuts as they swatted feebly.

Liana would pause, knife hovering, staring at the jars—cloudy with brine, mocking their labor. Fear gnawed at her: What if this never ends? What if something worse happens—another attack, a collapse—and she never sees her mom and dad again? Their faces flickered in her mind, distant and fading, as the onion fumes choked her hope. Yet they kept cutting, hands bleeding, and tears streaming—silent defiance in their exhaustion.

When they were finally allowed to return home, the bus jolted back to the city, its engine groaning under the weight of thirty silent girls, their hands scarred, eyes red from onion fumes and unspoken terrors. Liana stared out the window, the gray landscape blurring past—scorched fields, skeletal trees, and a sky heavy with lies. Her hands throbbed, cuts pulsating under makeshift bandages, the straw's prickle and the girl's bloodied scream still clawing her mind. The farmhouse's stench lingered in her hair, a ghost of that night's horror, when men had invaded their sleep, shattering innocence under a lone bulb's sickly glow. Liana's heart ached for home, for her mother's humming, her father's steady gaze, and the creaky flat offering sanctuary despite its poverty.

When the bus stopped, Liana stumbled into her parents' arms, their faces pale with anguish, the month's silence a wound they couldn't voice. Her mother's hands, trembling, cupped Liana's face, her eyes brimming with tears as she traced the cuts on her daughter's fingers, the skin swollen and raw. "My girl," she whispered, her voice cracking, leading Liana to the kitchen, where a chipped basin waited, filled with warm water and homemade salve. The scent of herbs, sharp and soothing, rose as her mother gently washed her hands, the water stinging before it calmed, each touch a silent apology for the cruelty that had stolen her childhood. Liana's father stood by, his war-scarred hands clenched, his gaze dark with a fury he dared not speak. "They worked you like slaves," he said, voice low, the words a vow against the iron fist. Liana nodded, tears spilling, the memory of the girl's torn shirt, her unconscious face, a weight she couldn't shake.

In their flat, modest yet still so lovely and welcoming, the air was thick with worries and despair. Liana sat, her hands bandaged, her mother's salve a thin shield against the pain. She thought of the labor camp's endless onions, the knives' dull glint, the men's drunken curses, and vowed to protect others from such horrors—her future children, her friends' children, and a generation unborn. The "noble tasks" were a lie, a chain forged to crush young souls, and Liana's defiance burned brighter, a fire kindled in the straw's prickle, a promise to fight for a world where no child bled under that boot. Her mother's touch, her father's silence, were anchors, but the scream of that night echoed, a call to carry truth forward, a spark she'd nurture in the years ahead.

FIZZ OF FREEDOM

The city sagged under a gray fist—streets cracked like old bones, smokestacks coughing grit, radios blaring lies about an "unbeatable" utopia. "Imperialism" was the favorite curse, spat like venom in classrooms, painting America as a drunken beast drowning in greed. A poster near the school gate showed an American soldier—uniform sloppy, Coca-Cola bottle jutting from his pocket, grinning like a fool who'd lost his map. They called it poison, a capitalist trick to rot pure souls. Liana, barely thirteen, envied that soldier's sloppy grin, craving a sip of that forbidden fizz under a sky free of spies. What kind of poison made you smile like that?

Her neighbor Peter, a wiry boy with wild eyes, had seen one of those red cans, smuggled by his uncle past the Iron Curtain's claws. Under a flickering streetlamp, they huddled, breath fogging in the chill, as he mimicked its pop—psshht—his hands dancing like a conjurer's. "It's not poison," he whispered, "it's freedom in a can." Their laughter burst out, quick and hushed, scattering at a neighbor's shadow. To kids like them, that can was a portal to a world they might never touch, colder than the snow clogging their boots. Liana clutched that dream, its fizz a promise she couldn't name.

Those Coca-Cola cans were part of a magical foreign land where life was different, as Liana saw them in the glossy images from the American Embassy displays in the city center. They gleamed with happy-looking people—families laughing, workers bustling—and impossibly tall buildings piercing the sky, their glass facades catching sunlight like a promise they couldn't ever touch. It wasn't just a building; it was a crack in their gray world, a whisper of something better beyond the Iron Curtain's chokehold.

Back in school, Liana and her classmates dreamed of America liberating them—tanks rolling in, not to kill but to save, a whisper from her childhood lodged deep in her heart. She still heard her father's voice, low over the radio's crackle in their cramped flat, his words steady despite the scars etched under his nails from the camps. "Every nation chooses its future, Liana—no one liberates you if you don't do it yourself," he said, his gaze piercing through the dim light, a truth that burned brighter than the lies blaring from the speakers.

Young and naive, Liana didn't yet understand that freedom must be forged, not just wished for. The taste of freedom grew stronger one day when she went to a movie with her friend Katya. They both wore minis; Liana's mother had reluctantly agreed to shorten one of her two skirts. It was a siren song from a distant land where people's wills were free, somewhere beyond the Iron Curtain that Liana strained to envision. Miniskirts and ponytails made both friends feel special, almost from the other side of the Iron Curtain, as they rushed to the movie theater. Mostly, Soviet films droned there, but this time, a French story beckoned, one they couldn't wait to savor.

As they walked, two policemen stopped them—one dragged Katya aside, the other shouted at Liana about her skirt. In a brief, nightmarish moment, the man stamped Liana's thighs, black paint covering her legs, damning her for trying to be a "rotten imperialist girl," while his partner cut Katya's ponytail, her golden locks dropping lifelessly to the ground. In horror, both girls fought the policemen, who held them tight, threatening them with prison. Liana struck one of the uniformed men, who threw her onto the asphalt, smashing her knee into a deep wound, blood streaming down her leg. People around stood quietly and obediently; no one intervened. It was a horrible, mind-altering experience, shaking both friends to their core. The policemen moved on, hunting for other rebellious juveniles, while Liana and Katya hugged each other, not realizing their resilience shone through.

The black paint clung to Liana's thighs like a brand, its acrid sting searing her skin as she stumbled away from the policeman's grip, Katya's severed ponytail a golden wound on the asphalt. Blood trickled from Liana's knee, the pavement's bite a deep ache, her miniskirt flapping like a flag of defiance in the cold dusk. Katya's sobs mingled with hers, their arms locked tight, a shield against the crowd's silent stares, obedient faces frozen in fear. The policemen's boots echoed down the street, hunting new rebels, their batons glinting under flickering streetlamps. Liana's heart pounded, rage and shame clashing—how dare they mark her, a thirteen-year-old girl, for a skirt that whispered freedom? The French film, its promise of glamour, waited in the theater, but the world felt smaller now, its gray walls closing in, the Iron Curtain's claws sharper than ever.

They pressed toward the theater, legs trembling, Liana's knee throbbing with each step, the paint a sticky humiliation drying in streaks. Katya's cropped hair caught the wind, her face pale but fierce, her eyes glinting with a fire that Liana recognized—her own defiance mirrored. The ticket booth loomed, its clerk squinting at their disheveled state, but Liana thrust their coins forward, her voice steady despite the tremor in her hands. Inside, the theater's dim warmth enveloped them, the screen flickering with a world where women wore minis without shame, their laughter free of Party spies. Liana sank into the seat, Katya beside her, their fingers intertwined, with the film's music a fleeting escape. But the paint's stench lingered, a reminder of the regime's reach, its eyes lurking even in this sanctuary.

Between scenes, whispers rippled through the crowd—older women, their scarves tight, leaned close, murmuring anger at the policemen's cruelty. "Why didn't you speak then?" Liana thought, her jaw tight, the silence of the street a betrayal that stung deeper than her knee. A man, his coat patched, offered a damp cloth, his eyes soft with pity, but Liana waved it away, the paint a badge now, a mark of her fight. Katya squeezed her hand, her cropped hair a crown of resistance, and they watched the screen, the French heroine's defiance echoing their own. The film ended, but Liana's resolve hardened, the theater's stale air thick with a vow: she'd never bow to their lies, their batons, their chains.

Back at school, the black stamp, the blue bruises on Liana's knee, and Katya's shorn locks became legends. Classmates buzzed, their whispers a hum of awe, their eyes wide as they crowded around in the courtyard, chalk dust swirling under their boots. "You fought the police!" a boy hissed, his grin sharp, and Liana felt a thrill, her heart swelling despite the ache. The school director's summons came swiftly, his office a tomb of Party posters, his voice droning propaganda as Liana's mother sat, her stony face masking her fear. "Your future's at stake," he warned, his pen tapping like a gavel, but Liana's eyes met Katya's across the room, their defiance a silent pact. Liana's mother endured the lecture with grace and patience, saying little, just nodding. At home, her mother's pleas—be obedient, stay safe—clashed with her father's quiet rage, his war-scarred hands holding her close, a lesson in truth over lies. That night, Liana lay awake, the paint's faint sting a reminder, her mind racing with dreams of a world where minis fluttered free, where

Coca-Cola's fizz wasn't poison but a spark of something brighter, a life she'd fight to claim.

Liana's father was an avid reader, with history books serving as his lifeline—especially those tracing politics and the world wars. After retiring, he'd vanish into them all night, pages rustling in their quiet flat. During the daytime, he'd huddle with friends, dissecting global news over chipped cups of coffee. Liana remembered him pressing Erich Maria Remarque's *All Quiet on the Western Front* into her hands, his voice low as he recounted World War II's horrors—a bomb cratering the neighbor's patio, shrapnel scarring their wall. Liana would sit, rapt, for hours, soaking in tales of a past that felt too close. Her father flew as an Army pilot in that war; his brother lost an eye to a head wound. War loomed in Liana's childhood as humanity's nadir—she feared and despised it, a shadow she couldn't shake. The regime fed that dread, bleating that the capitalist world—America, always America—would bomb them, raze them, and slaughter them. As a child, Liana would lie awake, heart hammering, until her parents hushed her: "No attacks, no bombs—it won't happen." Growing older, she saw through it—the fearmongering was to keep them cowed, obedient, and trembling under their boot. By her teens, the mask slipped. They lived in a "dictatorship of the proletariat"—Marx's malignant lie designed to seize production, and pool power in a one-party swamp. It was a true dictatorship, plain and brutal—dismantling capitalism across the Eastern European bloc with ruthless speed. Private homes—gone, nationalized. Control tightened—speech gagged, religion hunted, and lives tethered to the state's whim.

Their flat sat beside a hulking Stalinist printing factory—six stories of gray concrete churning out newspapers and books. At 4 a.m., trucks rumbled off, laden with propaganda—each page a polished lie, barely shifting day to day unless a fresh event needed sanitizing for their consumption. Reading between those lines became a matter of survival—judgment their only shield. One winter morning, Liana woke to a dark marvel—black flecks danced outside her window, crumbling midair, and dimming the sun. Wind spun them in a chaotic, ungodly waltz, dusting snow, homes, and streets with ash. She gaped, breath caught—then traced them to the factory's chimney. They were burning books! Her father confirmed it: a famed cartoonist's work had mocked the Party's leader—depicting him as a fat pig, the tail curled as his signature, captioned "Full Belly – Deaf to Science." Printed, sold, then seized —unsold copies torched. Liana later found one—the jab was sharp, true, and harmless. Yet the artist was punished, and his book became a collector's ghost. Books served power, not truth—hiding the regime's blood, its chains, its ruin. Ashes floated as a grim omen —history rewritten until they broke free. That morning, Liana stood at the window, ash on her fingers, her resolve hardening—she'd write her own truth, someday, somehow.

The country, once a land of thriving farms and golden fields, crumbled under communist and socialist rule, until food became scarce and hard to obtain. Feeding its own people became a struggle, a bitter irony for a nation that once exported abundance. Meat was a luxury they scarcely saw—imported, rationed, and doled out like a gift from the state. Once a year, lamb would appear in the stores, usually around International Labor Day. It was a rare treat, a fleeting promise of something better. That year, Liana's family waited eagerly, counting the hours. Her father braved a line that stretched for blocks, standing there for over six hours until he triumphantly returned with a few precious pounds. The entire family was giddy with anticipation. Liana's mother seasoned the lamb with care, roasted it until the kitchen filled with a rich, savory warmth that seemed to push back the grayness of their lives. She baked potatoes to a golden crisp and even made a cake—a small rebellion of joy. But first, they had the march.

May First dawned cold and gray. They rose early, dressing in silence, steeling themselves for the ritual ahead. Liana joined her school group, and together they trudged toward the Mausoleum, where the mummified body of their nation's first communist leader lay enshrined. Liana dreaded that place. The air inside was thick with the sharp, choking stench of formaldehyde, a smell that clawed at her throat. The leader's body, preserved under glass, had a sickly, transparent bluish tint to its skin, like a ghost trapped in time. It was grotesque, but they had no choice—school and university visits demanded they plaster on fake awe. Under his regime, countless people had been tortured or vanished into the night, yet there they stood, a generation forced to bow to his corpse. The guards' eyes followed them, cold and unblinking. Liana swallowed her revulsion, terrified not just for herself but for her parents—they'd already suffered enough for daring to whisper doubts about the socialist dream. Each step through those dim, echoing corridors was a battle to keep her stomach from turning, her face a mask of solemnity she didn't feel.

Outside, the relief was instant. The fresh air hit Liana's lungs like a lifeline, though the weight of those lies lingered, as heavy as the stench she'd left behind. At the Mausoleum's peak, a podium loomed, where the Communist Party elite stood in their crisp uniforms, gazing down at them—spineless sheep in their eyes, a herd marching to the blare of loudspeakers and hollow hymns of praise.

That May First, Liana's mind drifted from the mummy to the meal waiting at home. They waved their red flags, sang the anthems, and shouted their loyalty until the farce ended. Finally, she escaped to their little apartment. Her parents returned soon after, their faces weary but bright with the promise of the feast. They gathered around the table, the lamb's aroma wrapping them in a fleeting cocoon of happiness. Liana kissed their cheeks, her heart swelling with gratitude for their effort. They laughed, talked, and savored every bite—knowing this wouldn't come again for another year. It was a memory to cling to.

Hours later, that memory shattered. A faint unease crept into Liana's gut as they cleared the plates, a whisper she tried to ignore. Then it struck—sharp, searing pain that doubled her over. Her mother clutched her stomach, her face paling. Her father stumbled to the bathroom, retching. They had no idea that the meat, imported from Mongolia, had slipped through unchecked. No agency like the U.S. Food and Drug Administration existed there—just blind trust in a system that didn't care. Salmonella tore through them, and thousands more were affected. Hospitals overflowed, then turned people away, their halls choked with the sick.

For a month, Liana hovered between life and death. Fever blurred the days into a haze of sweat and delirium. When her father finally helped her from the bed, her legs buckled, and she crumpled to the floor. In the mirror, she didn't recognize herself—her face gaunt, eyes sunken, and bones jutting beneath sallow skin. She'd survived, but barely.

Years later, it happened again, but far worse. Alina fell ill—Liana's precious little one, born some years later, burning with fever, yet too weak to cry. Liana rushed her to the emergency room, but the doctors, their hands tied by a nationalized system, shrugged helplessly. "We can't help," they said. "You'll have to let her go." Medicine was free in name, but what good were educated doctors without drugs or tools? Desperate, Liana's mother called an old family friend, a gastroenterologist of rare brilliance. He'd written books, treated foreigners, and had ties to the elite—access to medicines they could only dream of. When he arrived, his face was grim but steady. "Leave the room," he told Liana, nodding to her mother to stay. Liana stumbled to the next room, sank to the floor, and prayed through tears that shook her whole body. He stayed all day. Liana pressed her ear to the door, catching the clink of glass and the murmur of his voice. As night fell, he called her in. There, between her pleas and his golden hands, a miracle unfolded—Alina's breathing steadied; her color returned. She would live.

Recovery was slow. The doctor prescribed vitamins, but finding them proved to be a nightmare. They sat behind the gleaming counters of "dollar stores," reserved for foreigners and the Party's inner circle only—bright havens of abundance the rest of them couldn't touch. Liana's mother's company had a German partner, and one of their representatives, a kind-eyed man with a soft accent, offered to help. Meeting him felt like a gamble—police could stop her, demanding answers—but Alina's life outweighed the risk. Inside the dollar store, Liana's head spun. Shelves gleamed with clothes, perfumes, even skis, in an impossible world. He bought five bottles of vitamins, and when Liana fumbled for her wallet, he stopped her. "Please, take care of your little one," he said, his voice gentle. "That's enough for me." Liana hugged him right there on the street, tears spilling, overwhelmed by this stranger's grace. Within a month, Alina was running again, her laughter a true blessing. Liana had been taught to hate the West, but the truth glared back at her: capitalism made the goods—medicines included—that socialism couldn't. A new fear gnawed at her—what if Alina fell ill again? What if no second savior appeared? How long could they endure this nightmare?

SEEDS OF DEFIANCE

The years following that miniskirt ordeal stretched into a blur of survival, Liana's teenage heart hardening under the Soviet boot. The black stamp on her thigh faded into a faint scar, but the fire it kindled smoldered, a quiet rebellion that the Party couldn't snuff out. School became a daily dance of deceit —chanting hymns to the Dear Leader while sketching Coca-Cola cans in her notebooks, her pencil a silent protest. The teachers droned on about socialist triumphs, their chalk dust settling like ash on desks scarred with rebellion, but Liana learned to hide her fight in plain sight, a skill that would serve her well.

The schoolroom's peeling walls closed in, Party posters curling at the edges, their red slogans screaming lies about capitalist decay. Liana sat at her scarred desk, her pencil tracing a Coca-Cola can in her notebook, its curve a silent protest as the teacher droned on about America's greed, her chalk dust settling like ash. The words stung—Liana's dreams of that forbidden fizz, sparked by Peter's whisper under the streetlamp, clashed with the teacher's venom. She clutched a smuggled Western magazine, its glossy pages hidden under her math book, a treasure Katya had slipped her during recess, its images of free girls in bright dresses a crack in the gray world. When the teacher barked, "Liana, name the imperialist threat!" her heart raced, defiance flaring.

"No," Liana said, voice low but steady, the classroom falling silent, with her classmates' eyes wide with fear. The teacher's face reddened, her voice shrill as she slammed her chalk on the desk, dust exploding like a storm. "You dare defy the Party?" she snapped, her glasses glinting like the principal's bayonets. Liana's hands trembled, the magazine's weight a secret burning under her fingers, but she held her ground. "America isn't the beast you claim," she said, her voice a spark, the words echoing her father's whispered truths. The teacher's hand shot out, grabbing Liana's arm, nails digging like claws, dragging her to the front. "Recite, or face the principal," she hissed, her breath sour with disbelief. Liana's knees shook, the memory of the miniskirt's black stamp searing her thigh, but she stayed silent, thinking of the magazine—a spark of freedom she'd carry, its pages a promise of a world beyond the Iron Curtain.

After school, Liana and Katya slipped to a park, the city's coal smoke stinging their lungs, with the gray streets fading behind skeletal trees. They sat on a splintered bench, sharing a stolen apple, its tart juice a burst of defiance against the meager rations. Katya's cropped hair, still short from the policeman's shears, caught the wind, her eyes fierce with the same fire that burned in Liana's chest. "I dream of America," Katya whispered, her voice low to dodge unseen ears, her fingers tracing the apple's skin. "No scarves, no slogans—just freedom to be." Liana nodded, her heart racing, the magazine's glossy images flashing in her mind—women laughing, skyscrapers glinting. "We'll get there," Liana said, her voice a vow, the apple's core a small rebellion they pressed into the dirt.

They spoke of escape, their whispers a shield against the park's shadows, where Party spies lurked in plain coats. Katya shared a story of her cousin, who'd fled to Vienna, his letters smuggled back with tales of music and light. Liana's thoughts drifted to her father's war stories, his scars a map of resistance, and she felt a special bond with Katya, their defiance a thread weaving them together. The park's chill bit their cheeks, but their laughter, quick and hushed, was a spark of hope, a promise to fight for a world where apples weren't stolen, where freedom wasn't a dream but a taste on their tongues.

One crisp morning, Liana walked with her father through the neighborhood's streets, the air sharp with the scent of coal smoke and damp stone, the city gray under a sky heavy with clouds. He paused before a picturesque two-story house, an architectural gem with stained-glass windows casting fractured rainbows on the cobblestones, its sloped roof extending over a welcoming porch carved with intricate vines. Century-old oaks surrounded it, their gnarled branches framing the house like a scene from a Christmas book, leaves rustling softly in the chill breeze. Liana's breath caught, her young eyes wide with wonder at its beauty, so unlike their cramped flat where walls sagged under the weight of lies.

"This was ours," her father said, his voice low, his scarred hands tucked into his coat, and his gaze distant with memory. "The communists took it when they came to power, handed it to a Party official who warms his boots on our hearth."

Liana's heart stirred, a mix of awe and ache. "We're so many in our tiny apartment, Papa," she said, her voice trembling with hope and a strange nostalgia for a life she'd never known. "This house is lovely—will they give it back to us?" Her small hands clutched his sleeve, the fabric worn thin from years of want. Her father smiled, a bitter curve that didn't reach his eyes, his scars glinting faintly under the morning light. "Maybe, one day in the distant future, not now," he said, and Liana felt the weight of his words, a pain that cut deeper than the cold. Their flat, its peeling walls and single stove, held six souls pressed tight, their dreams rationed like the bread they queued for. Why was this house, this piece of her family's heart, stolen? The question burned in her chest, a spark of defiance against the regime's lies.

Her father led her further, past the bakery's fleeting scent of yeast, to a large building of faded grandeur, its stone façade chipped but proud, windows glinting in the weak sunlight. "This was ours too," he said, his voice a whisper, as if the walls themselves might report him. Liana's jaw dropped—she knew this place. It was the health clinic her mother took her to when fevers gripped her or a toothache throbbed, its halls echoing with coughs and the clink of outdated tools. She'd never known it belonged to her father's family; its rooms once filled with their laughter, now a sterile maze where nurses shuffled under watchful eyes. The realization hit like a stone—on one hand, it was good that people had a place to heal, its walls a refuge for the sick; on the other, the injustice seared her, the contrast between her family's past and their present a wound that bled anew each time she passed its doors.

Liana stood frozen, her boots scuffing the cracked pavement, her mind reeling with the unfairness. Her father's family had once owned a sprawling vineyard in the northern hills, where he was born under skies wide with promise. She'd dreamed often of that land, its rows of grapes heavy with juice, a life close to nature, running free with animals, far from the city's gray chokehold. Those dreams crumbled when the communists seized it, nationalizing the land her grandparents had toiled for, their hands calloused from decades of care. Now, Party officials grew fat on stolen harvests, while Liana's family scraped by on rations, their plates as empty as their hopes. The clinic, the house—each was a theft, a monument to the regime's "justice," lauded as a gift to the people but paid for with her family's blood and sweat.

The walk home was silent, Liana's small hand in her father's, his scars a map of loss beneath her fingers. His coat—threadbare from years of use—barely shielded his weakened body from the biting wind. Liana squeezed his hand and made a vow: "One day, Daddy,

I'll buy you the warmest coat in the world." In their flat, a single bulb flickered, throwing shadows across bare walls. The air hung heavy with the scent of boiled cabbage. Liana's mother stirred the pot, eyes weary but soft. Liana wanted to scream—where was the justice for them? Her father sat at the table, his gaze fixed on a faded photograph of his uncle, a proud official executed by the regime's firing squad. "He spoke truth," her father said, his voice low, the words heavy with loss. "They called it treason, shot him after a farce of a trial, his blood a warning to us all." Liana's chest tightened, her fingers tracing the photograph's edges, its sepia a ghost of her family's past. Her great uncle's eyes, bright with defiance, mirrored her own, a spark kindled by that cruelty.

The communists called it a "just society," their posters screaming equality, but the expropriation of her grandparents' sacrifices, the seizure of homes and lands built over lifetimes, was a theft dressed in red flags. Her father sat, his war stories quiet now, his gaze fixed on a photograph of the vineyard, its faded green a ghost of what was lost. Liana's heart hardened, the spark of defiance kindled by that house's stained glass, the clinic's stone walls, growing into a fire. She'd carry this truth, a vow etched in her bones, to fight the lies that stole her family's past, a promise that would burn brighter in the dust of Cuba years later.

When Liana began her studies at university, she hoped to one day reach beyond the Iron Curtain with her diploma, achieving a lifelong dream of working in a free country. Studying literature was her goal; she dreamed of becoming a journalist, but this was unfortunately unattainable, as her family was "not progressive" by the regime's standards. They were branded bourgeois, capitalists—a damning label for those with the "wrong" past. They were seen as traitors, dangerous relics of a shameful history, who had to be isolated, reeducated, and silenced. Imagine living with that political sword of Damocles dangling overhead, day after relentless day—never knowing when it'd drop, only that it could, any moment.

Despite the propaganda that escaping the socialist paradise was a fool's dream—only arrest, prison, and a slow rot in some cell awaited dissidents in the West—despite the preaching that university diplomas were worthless there, Liana charged full speed ahead with her studies, holding in her heart the hope that one day she would become a writer, while in the meantime she chose to earn a civil engineering degree instead.

One year, Liana traveled to East Berlin, a rare chance to step beyond her country's chokehold. Excitement gripped her as the train rattled in—wheels clattering on worn tracks, the city pulsing, so close to the West, with the dreamland shimmering past the wall. She'd never felt freedom's edge so sharp. The S-Bahn hummed beneath her, vibrating through her bones, stations ticking by, each a heartbeat closer to West Berlin. She clutched her bag, her palms sweaty, the leather creaking, her mind tangled in longing and dread. Escape the socialist "paradise?" Every nerve screamed yes, but warnings—arrest, jail, and ruin—clamped like a vice, fear heavy as iron. She counted stops, her breath shallow, when the train lurched to a halt. Soldiers materialized—boots gleaming, with rifles slung low—on the platform. She froze, her heart slamming against her ribs. Were they East German or West? Uniforms blurred in panic—no insignia she could read, just menace in their stance. Prison flashed—cold bars, a life erased.

Trembling, she leaped off as the doors hissed shut, expecting shouts, hands on her wrists, or cuffs snapping tight. Nothing. Silence swallowed the platform, the air thick with her dread. She stumbled to the street, her legs weak, and glanced back—East German soldiers, who had stopped the last before freedom. Shame burned hot, a fire in her chest. She'd panicked, inches from the line, brainwashed into a coward by years of lies, their weight crushing her spine. East Berlin's gray streets stretched cold around her, a mirror to her battered mind. How long could she endure this—indoctrination grinding her down, turning her brain-dead? She needed an answer, fast, before she lost herself, her soul hollowed out.

That moment gnawed at her. Back home, she paced their cramped flat, walls closing in, creaking under her steps, Party slogans crackling from the radio—"The West is decay," "Loyalty to the Party is our life." As a kid, she'd parroted them, red scarf tight around her neck, saluting flags she didn't understand. Now, it was a noose—every lesson twisting tighter, threats coiling. She'd seen friends dull under it, eyes glazing as they nodded, their souls hollowed. Was she next? The question haunted her nights, sleep shredded by visions of soldiers, trains loaded with tanks, and a life beyond her grasp.

By twenty-two, love crept in like a rebel whisper. She met Marko, a young man with a warm smile, already holding a university diploma and a knack for joking about life's "golden shortages." Their courtship was a series of stolen glances across empty plates, sealed by a marriage performed beneath the unsmiling portrait of the communist leader—an uninvited guest who never left. The wedding cake was simple, with a smear of frosting—an unexpected treat. Liana's mother wept, not from joy but from fear of what lay ahead, while her father's hollow eyes hinted at pride he dared not show.

A year later, her daughter arrived, a tiny spark in a hospital room where hope was rationed. The walls peeled like the regime's promises, and the doctor—a weary man with shaking hands—muttered about "socialist care." Liana cradled her child, naming her Alina, a name that meant light, a defiance against the grayness. The joy was laced with dread, for the state's shadow loomed large. With a child on her arm, Liana finished university—earning the very degree the regime kept insisting was worthless anywhere beyond the borders of its socialist paradise.

Liana's new job was a maze of calculations and whispers, the office a gray cage under flickering bulbs, the air thick with cigarette smoke and Party privilege. The director's men—sagging suits, yellowed fingers—lounged in corners, their voices low, plotting favors for the elite. Their eyes followed Liana, their smirks sharp as the principal's bayonets from her school days, their whispers hinting at power that crushed without mercy. A secretary, her lips tight, warned Liana with a glance—stay quiet, stay small—but Liana's defiance, kindled by her father's scars, burned hotter, her heart racing as she sensed the director's gaze, a predator's glint she couldn't escape.

He was a powerhouse in the local Communist Party, his web sprawling across the city. Tall, broad-shouldered, he carried a strength worn thin by early gray hair and sagging skin. A cigarette hung constantly from his lips, smoke wreathing his face as one stub was swapped for the next, staining his fingers a dull yellow. Wrinkles etched his skin into a rugged mask—some might've called him handsome if not for the predatory smirk, the "I like you, so give in" glint in his eye. His voice thundered, commands barked like cannon fire, dentures clacking loose with every shout—a wet, metallic snap that curdled her gut.

Rumor swirled that he'd pursued all four women under his supervision—secretary, accountant, whoever crossed his desk. Now his gaze was fixed on Liana. Saying "no" wasn't smart—trouble brewed fast when you defied a Party man. No one to turn to, no help; the system shielded its own. Married, with a toddler at home, it didn't faze him. He started subtle—leers, offhand remarks—but her recoils only stoked his pursuit. In the open office, she'd bury herself in calculations, numbers swimming as his boots thudded near. His hand—rough, heavy—landed on her shoulder, a claim staked.

"How's the work coming along?" he'd growl, fingers pinching through her blouse. "Almost ready, Comrade," she'd mutter, twisting free, her voice taut. Futile. His arm locked tighter, pulling her close, his breath sour with tobacco and power. Day after day, the dance wore her down—his grip, her dodge—until he raised the stakes. "Get your calculations and come to my office," he barked one afternoon, eyes gleaming. Her stomach dropped. "This is it," she thought, her heart racing. She grabbed her week's manual figures—no computer for her; those were Party-only toys—and trudged to his office. The secretary's desk sat vacant, the accountant gone. A whiskey bottle glowed on his table, amber glinting through a half-open door.

"Sit down, Liana," he slurred, locking the door with a sharp click. Her heart pounded; he didn't care about her work. He poured whiskey, half a glass, grinning. "We can share." She stood, her voice steady despite the tremor. "Comrade, I need more figures from my desk," she said, inching back. He wasn't fooled. His hand slammed her shoulder, pinning her as he leaned close, his breath sour. "Calm down," he cooed, his grip tightening. Liana's defiance flared. "Don't touch me," she snapped, shoving him back. He faltered, startled—her resolve wasn't fake. "You'll regret this," he hissed, but relented for now.

Liana fled back to her desk, coworkers' eyes flicking to her, wide with worry, their lips sealed. Silence hung heavy—no one dared speak. Days later, he struck again. "Take your purse, we're leaving," he barked, towering over her. "Why? What happened?" she asked, her voice trembling, dread surging. "Job site issue—your fault. Come with me." A car idled outside, the engine humming. She slid in, hugging the door, but miles later, no job site emerged—just open roads veering to the outskirts. At a light, she grabbed the handle; he seized her arm. "Don't you dare," he hissed. "Want to lose everything?" His roar—"Drive faster!"—shook the driver, who stared ahead, mute. Fear clawed her, but defiance flared—she'd fight, whatever came.

An hour on, they reached a villa—one of the Party's plush retreats. Polished stone gleamed under manicured trees, the windows reflecting wealth. Inside, a couple bustled in a kitchen off a small dining room, the air thick with roasting meat and spice—luxuries she'd never taste at home. Their eyes met hers, soft with pity, but they stayed silent. The driver shifted, uneasy. Her boss led her to a room—no key, no lock—a sleek space, a bed plush with crisp sheets, a cushioned chair inviting rest. When she asked for another room, he didn't respond—his silence a wall. She perched on the chair, purse gripped tightly, cursing herself for not jumping out of the car in the city.

Dusk fell, shadows stretching long. They called Liana to dinner—plates piled with tender cuts, bread warm from the oven—but her stomach knotted too tight to eat. She stayed put, braced for the worst. A knock rattled the door—him, swaying, a whiskey bottle in one hand, and a Playboy magazine in the other. Its glossy sheen hit her like a slap; she'd only heard whispers of such things. Drunk, he lurched in, his pants half-undone. "You've been teasing me, refusing my fun," he slurred, his dentures flapping. "Utterly disgusting," Liana thought, then screamed, "Touch me, and I'll scratch your f---ing face!"

"C'mon, baby, you're a real cat—you excite me," he rasped, grabbing. She shoved, clawed—his face flushed crimson, his veins bulging. She prayed he'd collapse. No dice. He yanked her skirt; she shrieked—a raw, wall-piercing roar. Stunned, he faltered. "Don't you f---ing touch me!" she bellowed, raking his cheek. He cursed, smashed her head to the floor, then staggered out, the scratches bleeding. Dizzy, she slumped by the door, sobbing, blocking it with her body. No one came. Alone, terrified, she stayed awake, thirst gnawing, but too scared to roam the villa's halls for water.

At dawn, she snatched her purse and slipped out. The driver's voice halted her—"Get in." His gaze burned, furious. "Did that criminal hurt you? Force you?" "He didn't succeed," she choked, tears falling. He sped off, confessing he'd defied orders to return that night, haunted by what might've gone down.

Home, her father's face paled as she collapsed into him. "Papa, hold me," she sobbed. His arms—steady, warm—cradled her, his love washing away some pain. In the mirror, she saw her reflection —pale, neck bruised, a lump pulsing on her skull. Hot water stung, then soothed, rinsing tears and rage. Alina's voice piped up: "Mommy, where were you?" Liana locked the door—she couldn't let Alina see this wreck. Hours later, Alina fell asleep in her arms, her small breaths a soft light against the gray. The bruises from the villa faded, but the fire of her defiance burned brighter, fueled by the regime's lies—her family's stolen vineyard, the clinic's lost grandeur, and her father's scars. She thought of Marko, his steady hands sketching a future beyond the Iron Curtain, and vowed to protect Alina from the chains that bound her youth. The Western radio's static, hidden under her pillow, whispered of a world where freedom wasn't a dream but a right. Liana's heart hardened, her resolve a spark that would carry her to Cuba, where new battles awaited, the dust and heat a forge for her fight. She'd write her truth, a manuscript to break the silence, a promise for Alina's future, a beacon for all who dared to defy.

WITH ILLUSION AND HOPE

Liana and Marko ensured that their daughter, Alina, grew up happy and healthy, just as Liana's parents had raised her. Their small room became a home for three—Alina's giggles bouncing off the walls, sharp and bright against the damp gray, Marko's steady hand guiding her wobbly steps over cracked floorboards—while Liana's parents squeezed two tiny beds into the living room, their snores a soft hum through the thin curtain, a lullaby woven with her aunts' rustling. It was crowded, with seven of them—Liana, Marko, Alina, her parents, and her two last living aunts—crammed into a space meant for half that number, elbows knocking, breaths overlapping, but it was fun! They'd pile around the scarred table, passing dishes with beans and potatoes, laughing as Alina chased crumbs with sticky hands—her grin wide, eyes glinting despite the hollow ache in their bellies. They were hungry most of the time, with the pang a constant shadow through the night, but Alina made everything magic. She ran nonstop, her bare feet slapping the floor in a frantic patter, and talked nonstop—babbling tales of imaginary dogs and queens in high-pitched bursts—laughing nonstop, a bell-like chime that drowned out the gray seeping through the warped windows. Once, Alina grabbed her grandfather's cap, plopped it crooked on her head, and marched around, declaring herself "captain of the table"—they roared till tears streaked their cheeks, Liana's mother slapping the table so hard that it wobbled, her aunt's raspy cackle cutting through, her exile-worn voice a rare spark, a fleeting shield against the weight pressing in from the world.

That world outside their little oasis was not easy to navigate. With the increasing discontent among their compatriots—whispers snaking through bread lines like a slow hiss, fists clenched tight when nobody was watching—the regime's grip grew tighter, its hold a suffocating vise on their throats, squeezing till they gasped. News penetrated through the Iron Curtain more often—faint Voice of America crackles that Liana's father hunted at dawn, hunched over the radio like a thief in the dark, his breath held for a scrap of truth—making the government dial up the propaganda to hysterical levels, a shriek that drowned out any hope. "Socialist camp! Dictatorship of the proletariat!"—those words dogged their every step, plastered across the city, barked from loudspeakers till their ears rang, a relentless drumbeat of lies hammering them flat. They were told they were lucky to live in this camp—lucky for the hunger, the cold, and the fear—while the same socialist ideology marched through Hungary, Czechoslovakia, and Afghanistan—tanks rolling over cobblestones, lives snuffed in the dust, dreams buried under boots like theirs, heavy and unyielding. The air thickened with it—fear sharp as a blade, rage smoldering low, a tension they could taste in the stale bread, its crust cutting like the wind slicing through their thin coats.

Those years were the last gasp of a dying dictatorship—shouts from Berlin to Bucharest rattling their frail walls, a roar in their bones. The end was near, a faint light on the horizon—freedom's whisper, a crack in the gray—but hunger gnawed deeper, knocks grew bolder, and shadows stretched longer. Then Marko was sent to

Cuba. Guantánamo needed his engineering skills, they said—water contaminated, pipes leaking despair—with the American Naval Base looming right next door, its presence a silent threat. "You might have problems," they warned, faces blank, as if that masked the weight sinking into them like dampness.

While Liana was totally unprepared for what lay ahead—her bags stuffed with naive hope, socks and soap piled high, Alina's small hand sweaty in hers—she'd always be grateful to Cuba and its brave, wonderful people. Cuba made Liana who she was—tougher, sharper—forged her spine in its relentless heat, taught her to savor life's pulse, and to clutch every moment like a lifeline snatched from the void. It was the journey she needed to form her views, political and social, to peel back the mask of the socialist farce and see its grinning skull—teeth bared, eyes hollow—to arm herself with the strength to fight it tooth and nail, a fire lit under Castro's boot. That island broke Liana open, then built her back—stronger, fiercer, and alive—a woman who'd never bow again, her chin high where it once dipped.

Liana had never seen people so friendly, so vivid, and so in love with life as the Cubans were. Their smiles flashed through the cracks of oppression—bright, stubborn, a defiance she'd never known, a fire that burned where theirs had dimmed to ash back home. Often, Liana drifted back in memory, and despite the brutal moments they endured there—the hunger gnawing sharper than their potatoes, the heat pressing heavier than their damp flat, the fear cutting deeper than any knock—her heart swelled with appreciation for that country and its people, a warmth that lingered like their humid air on her skin, soft and clinging. They saw a land oppressed to a breaking point—streets crumbling into dust underfoot, shelves bare as graves—yet the Cubans found ways to smile, to live, to love and enjoy, a resilience that shamed their gray compliance, their heads-down trudge. Many times, facing life's inevitable bumps—bills piling like ration slips, problems creeping in like winter—Liana reminded herself it was a treasured gift, and she tried to be more Cuban in her views: savor it, move on, and let the sun burn through the cracks, a lesson their grins taught her.

Cuba gave Alina the gift of friendship—kids from different backgrounds, nationalities, and races—all blending in the dirt streets like a living quilt stitched with sweat and laughter. She didn't study diversity in school; it was everywhere—Cuban boys with gap-tooth grins trading marbles in the dust, a girl from Angola braiding Alina's hair with quick, deft fingers, and laughter crossing tongues in a chorus of joy that rang over the rubble. Alina never felt different, just one of them, chasing games through Guantánamo's dust—her squeals mingling with theirs, her bare feet kicking up clouds—loving them as brothers and sisters, her family bigger than their cramped flat ever could be. She grew up a happy child—sunburned cheeks glowing red, with endless chatter spilling like a brook—and that was all that mattered, her light a beacon slicing through the dark. Today, Alina volunteers her time, fighting for women in underdeveloped countries to have opportunities, to grow professionally, and to taste success—a fire that Liana knows Cuba ignited inside of her, a spark of justice born in those dusty streets, fueled by kids who shared her grin. Liana wasn't sure that was possible without those years; they shaped Alina, and Liana couldn't be prouder, her chest tight with pride, her throat thick with the weight of Alina's light.

As they prepared for their adventure, Liana and Marko were filled with the illusion that in Cuba, the regime would be nothing like the one they lived under—a lighter yoke, a softer boot, and a whisper instead of a shout cracking their skulls. Their naïve views gave them hope that travel would bring the freedoms they desperately prayed for—escape from the gray that stained their walls, the knocks that jolted them awake, and the lies that choked them like coal dust. Anything away from their country, appearing as salvation, seemed like a lifeline dangled just beyond the Iron

Curtain's edge, glinting in their dreams. Soon, Liana understood how oppressed they must've been to believe crossing borders to another socialist hell would make a difference—how deep the chains had sunk into their bones to make them grasp at shadows, mistaking them for light. They went to a much harsher world, where people were squashed under Castro's boot—crushed finer than dust, watched more closely than their whispers, and starved far deeper than their hunger ever dared.

On that October day, when Liana and five-year-old Alina took the plane to Cuba, Liana didn't know anything—just what Marko had told her after nearly a year living and working there, his voice a faint scratch over the line. "There's nothing here, please buy everything we might need," he'd said, crackling with distance and dread, a warning Liana couldn't fully hear. Nothing? Liana thought in their country they had little—potatoes stretched thin across seven plates, a rare chicken split till it was air—but nothing? Her mind couldn't grasp it, the word a hollow thud echoing as she packed soap, socks, and a doll for Alina—her hands trembling with illusion, her heart clinging to a fool's hope, fingers fumbling over the bags like they held freedom itself.

On their way to Cuba, they had to change planes in Madrid—a full day between flights. Liana got to see her aunt for the first time, her face a map of lines that Liana had only imagined. Her aunt had escaped when her father—Liana's great-uncle—was executed by the communists after the Red Army invaded, a bullet through his chest for his patriotism, his blood a stain on their march, a wound she carried across borders. She was the one who had sent Liana's father the life-saving medicine, smuggled by a cousin through shadows and bribes—vials that kept him breathing after the camp's torture tried to break him, his cough a ghost she fought from afar. She lived alone in Madrid, afraid to be in close contact with them—her letters as rare as rain, her voice a ghost over the years, faint with the weight of exile. And she was right! After picking them up from the airport, they noticed a car trailing them—black, sleek, too steady—following them all the way to her building, its engine a low growl behind them, a predator's hum. Liana's gut clenched, her hand tightening on Alina's till her chatter faded, with Liana's hiss sharp—"Who's that?" Her aunt's calm—"They always watch"—didn't ease the thud in Liana's chest, the fear spiking like a blade, but soon Madrid's architecture stole her breath—modern spires piercing the sky, glass gleaming like a promise, a far cry from their lifeless, squat panel blocks back home.

What a difference from her country! Liana was stunned by the city—an ode to eternal human genius, structures soaring like the American Embassy posters she'd craned to see as a kid, dreaming from behind the bars of their cage. And the people! Happy, serene, in clothes they could only dream of—colors bright as their laughter spilling into the streets, fabrics soft as a whisper brushing past—not the drab coats they patched for holidays, threadbare and stiff with wear. Liana's heart sank, bitterness flooding her like a tide—she tried to suppress it, to swallow it down, but it spilled out, a quiet rage boiling at the abyss between promise and reality, a chasm wide as the sky. All the lies, the futile propaganda they'd choked on, exposed in one quick glimpse beyond the curtain—a wound torn open wide, raw and bleeding, salt in every crack. Liana sat silently in her aunt's little car, pain and indignation burning as her eyes drank the truth—they'd been lied to, and knowing it wasn't enough; seeing it was a knife twisting deep, carving out the illusion. All Liana could think of was Alina, born into socialism's insanity—her giggles over that cap, her hands sticky with crumbs—and Liana swore, teeth gritted, hands clenched white, to do anything in her power to give Alina the life she deserved, a vow carved into her bones, a promise she'd bleed for.

Her aunt's building wasn't tall—five stories—but elegant inside, walls paneled in warm wood that glowed under soft light, every detail singing of a care she'd never known, a craft lost to their gray haste. "You live in a hotel?" Liana asked, her voice small, awed by the gleam that caught her eye. Her aunt smiled, soft and sad, "No, child, just a regular home." Her one-bedroom flat was a palace to Liana—clean lines cutting through the clutter of her life, a bed with real pillows plump with fine cotton. The food was alien—olives sharp and briny on Liana's tongue, cheese rich and strange melting in her mouth, bread that didn't crumble like dust under her teeth—and they had Coca-Cola! The fizz hit Liana's tongue, sharp and sweet, a burst she'd dreamed of since Peter's tales—Alina slurping beside her, wide-eyed, and giggling as bubbles tickled her nose. Liana felt rich and poor at once, a queen in rags, the cold can a treasure in her grip. They talked of Liana's parents, her aunt's exile—her aunt's voice steady, regal, and carrying the weight of years as Alina played with a new doll, a gift clutched tight, its plastic arms a treasure she hugged close. Liana showed her aunt her prom photos, the dress made from her aunt's fabric, a faded thread of her care—her aunt's eyes softened, a flicker of the past they shared lighting her face. Her aunt's regal air, free of Liana's worried crease, held her like an anchor—happy in Madrid, the nightmare behind her, and a life she'd wrested free from the jaws of their past. When her aunt said, "You can always stay," holding Liana close, her warmth a pull that sank into Liana's skin, temptation roared—freedom here, now, a breath from the curtain's edge, a life unshackled. "I can't, Auntie," Liana choked, her throat tight, and tears burning behind her eyes. "They'll arrest my family, ruin their lives." The pull tore at her, a rip in her chest, a scream she swallowed—but she turned away, her aunt's embrace a ghost on her skin, lingering as they left.

The next day was their flight to Havana, Cuba. Rules were lax then—Liana boarded with seven carry-ons slung over her shoulders, two suitcases filled to the breaking point, Alina in tow, her chatter a lifeline threading through the chaos of the terminal. Flight attendants, kind-eyed under tired smiles, stowed their bags overhead with quick hands, walked Alina around the cabin—her squeals a balm as she pointed at clouds through the scratched window, her doll bouncing in her grip, its head bobbing with her glee. At José Martí Airport, humid air streamed through vents as they landed, a strange, thick smell filling the cabin—wet earth, salt, a caress—as they stepped out onto the tarmac, the heat wrapping them softly and suddenly. The sun rose, fierce and blinding—Liana shut her eyes against its glare, breathing deep, her first taste of the tropics—warm, gentle, and a hug she didn't expect, soaking into her bones. Since then, Liana has chased warm places—sun scorching her skin till it stings, humidity wrapping her tight like a second skin, long summers stretching endlessly—shunning cold, craving that soft dawn like a memory she couldn't shake, a pull that never faded.

That joy snapped short at customs—grotesque, a gut-twist that stole Liana's breath and left her reeling. They tore through her bags, hands pawing every shirt with rough fingers, flipping every book page like they hunted secrets—suspicion glinting in their eyes, their voices sharp as knives cutting through Liana's hope, slashing it to ribbons. The bubble gum her aunt gave her—a dream back home, a rare, sweet burst Liana had saved—was snatched from her grip, their fingers snagging it like thieves; Alina's peach, half-eaten, was ripped from her mouth midbite, juice dripping down her chin. Alina wailed, "Mommy, why?"—tears streaking her cheeks, her voice a stab through Liana's chest as she fumbled to repack, her hands shaking, and their glares boring into her like she'd smuggled a bomb, not soap. Exhausted, Liana fought her own tears, swallowing hard, the lump a stone—then they were out, Alina running to Marko, with her arms wide open, "Daddy, they took my peach!" Kisses rained down, hugs fierce and tight, and Marko's arms a shield after a year apart—love swirled, steadying Liana, his laugh a rope pulling her from the edge, his voice a balm over Alina's sobs.

They stayed a week in Havana at Marko's friend's home—not a hotel, he said; those were grim, water trickling scarce from rusted taps, a drip, not a flow. Walking the streets felt like a time machine had yanked them back—old American cars, 1930s relics with chipped paint, rumbled past, engines groaning like tired ghosts dragging their chains; Soviet Ladas coughed rust in the humidity, their frames pocked with holes, wheezing through the thick air, a death rattle on wheels. Cafeterías offered café Cubano—strong, sweet, a jolt that cut through jet-lag fog, served in chipped cups that burned Liana's lips—but stores rationed all else: one lingerie piece per woman, every two years, threadbare and gray, a scrap not a shield. A shop's dusty shelves held only butterfly floaties—frog-green, yellowed, and plastic sagging—a nightmare Liana couldn't shake, next-level poverty etched in her skull like a brand, a scar that wouldn't fade. "Nothing" meant nothing—no food beyond crumbs they'd fight rats for, no hope beyond dust that choked the air, just a void staring back, hollow and unblinking.

Old Havana left Liana stunned—there was only one way to describe what she saw—ruins. Once beautiful, the Spanish colonial-style buildings were literally falling apart—plaster peeling in wet clumps, balconies sagging like broken wings, and a faint whiff of mold stinging her nose. After witnessing the magnificent architecture of Madrid—its spires sharp, its gleam eternal—this felt gut-wrenching, a punch to Liana's chest. She got scared; a feeling of impending doom overpowered her—her breath caught, Alina's chatter fading as the unknown reared its ugly head, a shadow curling over them. Between the illusion that Cuba was salvation and the hope that it'd bring freedom—dreams Liana had stitched into those seven carry-on bags—they braced for Guantánamo, eyes open, hearts bruised, the lie laid bare, raw and bleeding in Havana's dust.

GUANTÁNAMO CITY—
TEARS, DUST, AND POVERTY

With sighs, pops, and creaks, the car shuddered to a stop at a house Liana, Marko, and Alina would call home for a few unforgivable years—its engine wheezing like an old man's last breath, a death rattle in the heat. The exhausted Soviet Volga, paint chipped to a dull gray, barely conquered the distance from Mariana Grajales Airport to this Guantánamo neighborhood—a cluster of squat, weary houses nestled among the usual socialist sarcophagi, those looming concrete hulks staring down like tombs, stained with years and salt. One hundred Eastern European specialists lived here, shipped in to stitch up Cuba's fraying seams—unfiltered water, pipes weeping—and this was their patch of dust and despair, a gritty haze swirling as they rolled in. All around was dirty—grit caked the cracked pavement, danced in the humid air, and settled thick on rooftops sagging under a merciless sun. A Cuban kid waved, gap-toothed, from a stoop—dust puffing under his feet—but Liana couldn't force her facial muscles into a smile for his sake, stiff with jet lag, and tight with dread creeping up her spine. Alina stood nearby, her doll nestled in her arms, blue eyes curious, and blonde hair sticking to her sweaty neck.

People from Marko's office spilled out—remarkably friendly faces, sun-worn and grinning, their voices a warm jumble Liana couldn't catch, fast and rolling like the sea nearby. They chattered, hands waving—calloused, quick—eyes bright with a welcome that cut through the haze, a lifeline in the grime. Liana tried to join in, thanking them for the warmth, dusting off her fluent Italian—"*Grazie, molto gentile*"—hoping it'd bridge the gap, her tongue steady but unmoored in this Spanish-speaking world. They blinked, puzzled, then burst into laughter—a rolling, generous sound that cracked Liana's shell open, their heads thrown back, their teeth flashing. Marko grinned, shrugging, and they raised worn glasses in a toast to friendship, clinking them high, a sharp tink against the Volga's creak. The ice broke, a fleeting melt in the heat, and Liana felt a flicker of something soft—human, alive. This would repeat over the years they spent there—those Cuban friends, loyal through the hard times when the Secret Service trailed them like dogs, their shadows long and lean, when they'd scribble notes at home to dodge their ears—sharp, unseen—breathing strength into Liana when hers ran dry, their hands steady on her shoulder.

More folks trickled in, some towing kids—gap-toothed, barefoot, a swirl of white, yellow, chocolate, and black skin under the sun, dust kicking up around them. Liana couldn't believe the happiness and exaltation blooming on Alina's face—her blonde hair bouncing as she darted toward them, her serious mask from back home gone, shed like a skin that had been much too tight. Too often there, Alina's face had mirrored Liana and Marko's—stern, pinched, and feeling the tension and fear that clung to them like damp, a shadow she couldn't name. Here, that fell away—language didn't matter; Alina chattered in her own way, a mix of squeals and wild gestures, and they answered back, a universal kid-code of grins and games—tag, hops, and a dance of dust. Liana's heart swelled, watching her—an amazingly heartwarming picture of children playing cheerfully, finding the peace adults couldn't scrape together, their laughter a rope across the void. Right there, among those kids, Alina, with her blue eyes and blonde hair, started to grow, knowing they were all equal—dust and giggles binding them tighter than words, a truth her five years hadn't yet learned to doubt.

Liana ventured outside—dust everywhere, a gritty haze choking the air, stinging her eyes, and just a few palms and cacti spiking up around the houses, their spines defiant against the void. The four- and five-story buildings loomed uglier than those back home—squat, stained concrete shells with crooked wood blinds gaping wide at windows and balconies, with no glass to keep out the heat, just slats rattling in the breeze. No place had air conditioning; the sun was merciless, a hammer pounding down, the humidity suffocating, a wet rag plastered over Liana's face. People passed by, friendly and inviting—words tumbling from their lips that Liana couldn't catch, smiles she could feel—trying to talk, their hands waving her closer, a call through the haze. Liana wondered how they found happiness in this misery—dust clotting their hair, heat baking their skin raw—yet their clothes were immaculate, fresh from some unseen laundry despite the grime, a sweet powder scent cutting through like a whisper of care, a secret Liana couldn't crack, a mastery she couldn't match.

By afternoon's end, everyone drifted off, voices fading into the heat like a tide pulling out. Tired from the travel—bones aching from the plane's hard seats, skin sticky from the day's swelter—Liana, Marko, and Alina looked around. The house wasn't big—three small rooms, walls stained with years of neglect, a living area with a kitchen squeezed in, its countertop cracked—but it was theirs, not a corner of Liana's mother's flat. For the first time, they had a home, a space to breathe—or so Liana thought. Her happiness flared, a brief spark lighting the gloom—then turned to horror as she twisted the faucet. Brown water sputtered out, murky as swamp mud, stinking faintly of rust and rot. Liana had forgotten the warning—boil it, shower with mouths shut—and the spark died fast, snuffed by the stench. Horror turned to panic that night when Liana jolted awake to dozens of roaches—crawling, skittering, and some flapping their wings like drunken flies—swarming the floor and the walls, a black tide surging in the dark. Liana swatted, gasping, a scream caught in her throat—Alina tumbling as Liana yanked her close, her small body warm against Liana's pounding chest.

Liana spent the rest of that night drowned in tears, self-pity pooling—she, a puddle of regret, her sobs a low hum against the walls still foreign to her—her parents' flat a palace in her mind, her mother's soft hum and her father's steady gaze desperately unreachable when Liana needed them most. Then, at dawn, a jet roared low—too low—shaking the house, rattling the thin panes till they sang; Liana screamed, tumbling half off the bed, her body trembling, the floor cold against her palms. Alina stirred, whimpering—Marko bolted up, his voice sharp—"It's the base, just miles off; you'll get used to it." "No," Liana snapped, tears hot, "I want to go back, I'm not living here with her like this." Marko froze, desperate between Liana's resolve and the sticky trap they'd landed in, his hands grasping for words that wouldn't come.

They stepped onto the terrace, the air still thick. In that instant, the buildings faded—the misery, the distress blurring out. Everything was dark, then above their heads, the sky cracked open, brightening fast—just after a cloudy shroud, the palms, flowers, and birds began to shine, a burst of green and red against the gray. God, what an immense beauty—colors sharp, no half-tones, every hue intense, strong, and full of life, like paint spilled fresh from a can. Liana's eyes, tired from the gray monotony of her native city, couldn't deny themselves anything but this—nature flaring alive, a jolt through her veins. She felt something unusual—unknown happiness and tranquility she hadn't tasted in years, a calm settling deep within. "I think we'll be fine here," Liana said, her voice soft, "Forget that I asked to leave." They weren't ones for show—emotions locked tight—but Liana hugged Marko hard, his shirt damp against her cheek, his breath a steady anchor.

This is how Liana began her life in Guantánamo, Cuba—tears drying, resolve hardening. In the following days, her eyes opened to the real Cuba—not the newspaper lies from home, but a raw, unfiltered truth. Her first impression held—total misery, poverty's claw—but she saw more: Cubans in poor, clean rags, balconies strung with washed tatters, a stubborn pride in every thread. The ugly construction didn't shock—back home, architectural fantasy was chained too, Liana's designer's eye dulled to it. Near them, another Eastern European family's house bloomed with flowers—a garden one man carved from dust. Liana decided then—she'd fight this dirt. Finding a hoe or pickaxe was a bust; soon she gripped a machete, hacking at the filthy mix of dust, dirt, and construction junk around their house. Cubans watched—smiles wide, doubts quiet—as Liana swung, sweat stinging her eyes. It took a week, her shoulders and back blistering red, then bursting raw—she hid inside for days after, her skin peeling angrily, but she triumphed.

Liana and Alina collected seeds, planted, and watered—drove a pole behind the house, and watered again. Soon, climbing beans cloaked it, flamboyant trees murmured, their fiery flowers blazing, palms swayed with thorny sycamore leaves, and that stick grew into a guava tree—village kids climbing its branches, hunting fruit, their shouts a song. But a few years later, Liana would destroy it—rip it bare, the house stark in the dust again—her brain and heart wrestling a strange homicide that taught her their fate often lay in others' hands, not always kind, a lesson that'd blind her to beauty and ruin.

The morning after their arrival, a Cuban neighbor, Rosa, knocked softly, her hands clutching a worn clay pot, steam curling with the scent of black beans and rice, a gift in Guantánamo's scarcity. Her smile, warm as the sunbaked concrete, eased Liana's dread, her eyes kind despite the hunger lines. "*Para la niña,*" Rosa said, nodding toward Alina, who stood nearby, her doll nestled in her arms, her blue eyes curious. Liana's throat tightened, the gesture a spark in the sun. They sat on the stoop, the concrete cool, but words faltered—Rosa's rapid Spanish blurred, while Liana's Italian, fluent from years of study, found no echo. "*Grazie, molto gentile,*" Liana ventured, gesturing to the pot. Rosa's brow furrowed, then her laugh rang, her hands miming eating, pointing to Alina, who giggled, waving her doll. They traded fragments—"*bambina, felice,*" "*comida, amor*"—Liana's Italian weaving with Rosa's Spanish, their hands dancing, their eyes locking in shared intent, their laughter a bridge across the chasm. Rosa's tales of her children emerged in broken phrases, Liana responding with stories of snow, her Italian lilting, pieced together with nods. The effort forged a bond, Liana's resolve hardening for Alina. Rosa's hand, calloused but gentle, squeezed hers, a promise of friendship to endure Guantánamo's trials, a spark of community that burned against the odds.

Days rolled on—Marko at work, Liana wrestling the house, and Alina settling smoothly into this dust world. A photo lingered: Alina and her first Cuban sister, dark curls brushing blond, staring into each other with a love that needed no translation. Alina babbled Spanish fast—progress sharp—her sickly city pallor gone, replaced by the ruddy flush of outdoor life. Mornings, she'd leap from bed, scarf breakfast on the stoop—waking friends with a yell—play sparking instantly. Afternoons, she'd dodge naps with twenty excuses, nights collapsing wherever sleep caught her—sprawled on the floor, with her doll nestled close. Liana felt happy—childhood was unspoiled here, not caged by city gray. Alina grew stronger, her hair blonder under the sun, and swimming soon—proud as she splashed. They'd hit the beach in their Skoda Octavia—frog-green, seats torn like they'd wept for years, a rattling beast that shattered nerves with its roar, a miracle that it ran at all—their first car, a defiant jalopy in this kingdom of poverty.

That first morning, when Liana swore to make this Cuban mess work—five or six kids spilled into her new home, rags clean but poor, hungry eyes widening at cheese from their rattling fridge, a treasure to them. Shame twisted her—for having more, for chances they'd never touch. Close by, the "supermarket" mocked its name—ugly packages thinning out, stalls emptying to echoes.

The next day, Liana ventured to the "supermarket" with Alina, the concrete path gritty under their sandals, the air thick with dust and the tang of overripe fruit. The market was a squat building, its walls peeling like empty promises, with its shelves sparse under flickering bulbs. Cubans crowded the aisles, ration cards gripped tight, eyes scanning for scraps—rice, beans, or a rare slab of meat swarmed by flies. They snatched their share from open boxes, a black cloud buzzing—but hunger blinded them; they didn't flinch. Liana gagged, the only one seeing the filth. Those shameful cards—rationed scraps doled out—scared her: fridges with water only inside, American relics of former abundance, now hollow. How many endured with optimism, how many with regret? Liana couldn't tell—but none foresaw the crueler trials ahead.

Liana's stomach churned, the stench of decay a slap after her Eastern European markets, where hunger was familiar but less raw. Alina stayed close, her doll nestled in her arms, eyes wide at the chaos, the buzzing black cloud a threat Liana couldn't shield her from. She handed over their coupons, fingers trembling, and received a small bag of rice—grains flecked with grit, a mockery of sustenance. A woman beside her, her dress patched but clean, offered a smile, her hands quick as she tucked away her rations. "You're new," she said, Spanish warm, eyes kind despite the hunger etched in her face. Liana nodded, her throat tight—the woman's resilience a mirror to the Cubans who'd welcomed them. "It's always like this," the woman said, gesturing to the empty shelves, her laugh a defiant response to the void. Liana's heart ached—her family had more, their foreign status a thin privilege, but the shame burned, a reminder of her stolen vineyard back home. The market's filth and the flies' relentless hum seared into her mind, the woman's smile a spark against the gray. She recalled the miniskirt's black stamp, her father's scars, and the injustice of ration cards—chains of hunger, weapons of control.

That night, as Alina slept, her small breaths a rhythm against the hum of distant jets, Liana sat by the dim glow of a lamp, the cracked table anchoring her thoughts. The concrete floor, cool under her feet, steadied her as memories surged—Guantánamo's contrasts clawing at her heart: the poverty that gnawed, the flies that mocked their hunger, and the warmth of Cuban smiles that lit the dust like stars. Her thoughts drifted to Marko, his silence growing since their arrival, with his late nights a wound she couldn't name, a shadow heavier than watching eyes. The market's stench, the woman's laugh, mingled with memories of her Eastern European past—the miniskirt's black stamp, her father's scars—now joined by Cuba's grit and hope. Alina's laughter, a defiance against the grayness, fueled Liana's resolve, yet fear lingered that this island would break them, as their homeland had tried. She vowed to protect her daughter and carve a truth no one could silence, a spark burning brighter in Cuba's heat.

Out there was Guantánamo Bay, hemmed by barbed wire, threats lurking, and eyes watching every step they made.

SAME IDEOLOGY, DIFFERENT SOIL

How many people endured the hardships with optimism —or simply with deep, gnawing regret? Liana didn't know, but no one wanted to imagine the future might subject everyone to greater, crueler trials—a shadow creeping closer, heavier than the dust they breathed. Liana never understood why the Cuban people didn't rebel against the oppression that had crushed them for decades—decades of no food beyond scraps, no clothing but rags, no freedom to speak, no hopes to cling to, no dreams to chase, just fear and misery grinding them into the dirt. Back in school, Liana and her classmates dreamed of America liberating them—tanks rolling in, not to kill but to save, a whisper from her old school that stuck deep. She still heard her father's voice, low over the radio's crackle: "Every nation chooses its future, girl—no one liberates you if you don't do it yourself." His words burned then, burned now—a truth she hauled across borders, a weight in her chest. The lie was the same in her country and Cuba —a glittering promise destined to collapse in hunger and dust. Yet Cuba had edges that her land didn't: close to the United States, the

American Naval Base squatting on its soil, a taunt of help within reach, a lifeline her family couldn't dream of behind their Iron Curtain, far from any savior's shore.

The municipal city of Guantánamo sat 15–20 miles north of the bay's edge—not hugging it, but close enough to feel its pull. And to hit a beach, Liana, Marko, and Alina had to claw through those miles of road—every inch a Cuban military zone, barbed wire snarling from both sides like jagged teeth, glinting under the sun. Liana could only guess it caged the American base, a shadow beyond the thorns. Signs stabbed up at every step—"Mines Ahead, Shooting to Kill"—their faded paint a scream in the silence, a sharp twang when the wind snapped the wire taut. For years, Liana felt invisible eyes tracking them—wherever they went, whatever they said—prickling her neck, a ghost she couldn't shake, and a hum she couldn't unhear. At the start of their Cuban life, the communist regime still called them "brothers"—foreigners, sure, but comrades, watched closely with a smile that didn't reach their eyes. After Eastern Europe's socialist bloc crumbled—Berlin's wall dust, Bucharest's roar—Castro's hysteria hit a fever pitch; in a heartbeat, Liana and Marko, and even little Alina, turned dangerous, a threat to their rotting stronghold, their "brother" badge swapped for a target, their steps louder in their ears.

They weren't yet "enemies of the revolution" that day—still weaving between barbed wire, mine warnings, and kill shots, Liana, Marko, and Alina could snatch pleasure in expecting the beach, a weekend's gasp amid the dust. The miraculous Skoda fought the hills—its coughing engine hacking like a smoker's last drag, axles groaning with a sad history of snapping—carrying them up, Marko's pride in its frog-green hide unshaken, a grin creasing his sun-burnt face. They stopped to snap pictures—Liana's parents back home, itching to see Alina bloom on tropical soil, her blonde hair wild in the sun, a burst against the gray they knew. The road stretched empty—no cars, just dust and cacti spiking through the haze, their spines glinting like knives. Alina ran back and forth, chasing butterflies—wings flashing yellow, her squeals cutting the quiet—while Liana aimed her camera at a palm, its fronds sharp against the sky. Then Liana froze—behind it, a building loomed, uniforms staring down, astonishment twisting their faces into knots of concern. Cuban military—close, too close—and Liana had nearly clicked the shutter, lens pointed where it shouldn't be. She dropped the camera fast, and waved—a shaky, dumb grin plastered on her face—and they bolted, Alina's doll bouncing as Liana yanked her in, dust kicking up behind them. Arrest loomed—Liana wouldn't have blinked if they'd stormed their door, boots thudding. Joy shattered; their "brother" shield evaporated, a fool's hope gone in a breath. For days, every knock jolted Liana—her heart hammering, expecting cuffs and shouts—but it didn't come. Years later, post-bloc fall, they'd have nabbed her—her camera seized, and grilled her over her "curiosity"—no doubt, no mercy, just a cell's cold slap.

Days rolled on, and the work Liana and Alina poured into the garden bore fruit—tropical soil, fertile as a gift, bloomed fast under God's sun, sticks sprouting despite dust and debris choking the ground. Palms flared green, beans climbed wild, and flamboyants blazed red—yet the stores sat near-empty, a cruel, mocking jest. "There is nothing in the shops," a neighbor muttered, her voice flat, "but the private market's got bananas, mangoes, and tomatoes—pricey, though." Same as home, Liana thought—always failing, no matter the soil, no matter the sun. Apple, SpaceX, Tesla—none could've breathed here, choked by rules that strangle ingenuity, and starve it dead. What stunned Liana most: some in the U.S. still didn't see it—blind to history's lessons screaming from Cuba's dust, her country's gray—refusing the truth they bled for, a refusal that clawed at her gut.

Greater shame seized Liana the first time she stepped into the local grocery for foreign engineers and specialists—meat, cheese, salami, and oil, a bounty Cubans couldn't touch, stacked high behind locked doors. They got weekly slabs—more than a Cuban family saw in months—while their kids gnawed at hunger's edge, ribs poking through. Horrible injustice—their land, their hands growing it, yet barred from its taste, their eyes hollow when they passed. It echoed back home, hunting vitamins for Alina—poisoned by bad food—when a German man took Liana to a dollar-only store, her mother's work connection her key, her mother's moans a ghost in her ear. Liana and Marko started inviting Cuban friends to dinner—sharing meat, a frail pay-it-forward—Marko slicing salami thick, their eyes wide as plates, a quiet "Gracias" slipping out, cutting deeper than knives. But the rest? Millions of kids—bloated bellies, parasite-riddled, with starving eyes sunken—Liana couldn't reach, her shame a stone sinking, her rage a fire licking at a system hoarding from its own, a theft dressed as justice.

May First dawned—International Workers' Day, like back home, but more stringent—at least Liana and Marko didn't have to endure those Castro rants, weren't forced to hang portraits of the communist "dear leader" glaring from their walls. Cubans hung his face in every home—a reminder of who ruled, Liana guessed—mandatory ears for his hours-long, unhinged screeds, hate spewing from every TV, a venomous drone promising prosperity's echo while imperialists loomed as villains, his voice a lash on their backs. Exhausted souls—poverty-worn, hunger-thin—clapped, with vigilante eyes and ears poised to snitch on any flinch, a mirror to the Soviet leaders' cult, a trap Liana knew too well. At first, Liana listened—her country's papers cast him as alpha, hero, king—curiosity piqued, ears open. Soon, it turned to rage—Guantánamo, socialism's poster child, mocked his lies with every dust-choked street, every empty shelf, a slap to his "triumph" louder than his words.

That first time Liana saw Guantánamo in daylight, it hit her—one afternoon they'd decided to explore the city, leaving their dusty patch behind. A human cordon blocked the Skoda—screams and sobs piercing the haze, a mother clutching a fevered child, two hours she'd been begging for a ride, her voice raw with despair, her arms trembling under his weight. No phones, no transportation—just dust and pleas—they took them, racing to a hospital clogged with the sick—sweat, moans, hours of waiting ahead, and a line snaking into shadow. That day, with the sick child writhing in pain and fever beside Alina—his sweat damp on her arm, her doll pressed tight—Liana prayed it wasn't contagious, her gut twisting as she watched him retch, helpless. Liana couldn't imagine then that a fragile life would be born in that same rattling Skoda—its frog-green shell a womb—when a father pounded their door one night, his wife hours into labor, no help, no way out, her gasps an empty plea through the dark. She birthed there as Marko floored it to the hospital, blood streaking the torn seats, her wail a miracle amid the engine's roar—a moment Liana would clutch, as proof that life fought through the ruin, a spark in the dust.

But that first day in Guantánamo's glare, something slammed Liana's gut—the world swirled, a horror she couldn't name, bile rising fast. Roads dust-coated—asphalt a rumor—kids naked, bellies swollen, parasites gnawing inside, houses gasping their last, and poverty screaming from every crack, every slant. Was this Castro's "triumph?" It looked like Africa's poorest fringe, not a revolution's crown—mud and flies, not glory. Back home, Liana broke—sobbing, yelling at the walls—how criminal to drown in this and trumpet socialist "success" on screens, lies thick as the dust? Liana didn't know then that she'd see worse—crimes piling in tyranny's name, a shadow stretching long, dark as the mines beyond the barbed wire.

Something wasn't right between Liana and Marko, a fracture creeping into the humid air of their Guantánamo shack. Soon after their arrival, the dust still settling on their sparse belongings, Liana noticed Marko's late returns from work, his footsteps heavy on the creaky floor, his eyes distant as if lost in a haze thicker than the Cuban sun. When she spoke to him, her voice soft over the clink of chipped plates, Marko seemed elsewhere, his responses clipped, his gaze drifting past her to the cracked walls. Even Alina's hugs, her small arms fierce around his neck, her kisses sticky with mango juice, failed to coax a smile from his face, which remained a mask carved from the same gray stone of their Eastern European past.

Liana's heart twisted with worry—perhaps the strain of his engineering work, patching Guantánamo's crumbling infrastructure under the regime's watchful eyes, consumed him. She asked, her voice tentative, if the blueprints piling on their wobbly table were the cause, but Marko brushed her off, his sigh heavy with unspoken burdens. One night, as the cicadas droned outside, he declared he needed more sleep, the bed's sagging mattress too narrow for two. "Sleep with Alina," he said, his voice flat, his eyes avoiding hers. Liana froze, the words a slap, her chest tightening as if the room's humid air had turned to ash. Their bed, once a haven of whispered dreams … now a chasm between them. Days later, the sting deepened when wives of Marko's coworkers, their eyes sharp with gossip, cornered her at the market, their voices low under the palm fronds' rustle. "Is it true that you don't share a bed with Marko?" they asked, their pity laced with judgment, a scandal in the eyes of passionate Cubans who wove love into every gesture. Liana's face burned, her hands clutching a rationed loaf, the marketplace's chatter a blur as she mumbled a denial, her heart sinking under the weight of their stares.

They lived together in separate orbits, their roles carved by necessity in Guantánamo's dust. Marko rose at dawn, his boots scuffing the floor, as he secured meat, rice, and beans for the table.

His status as a foreign specialist was a lifeline in a land of empty shelves. Liana crafted comfort in their shack, sweeping grit from the corners, sewing patches on Alina's worn dresses, her hands steady despite the ache in her chest. Their conversations dwindled, replaced by the hum of a battery-powered radio, its static a faint echo of the forbidden broadcasts she'd once hidden under her pillow. The silence between them grew, a shadow heavier than the island's relentless heat.

One evening, as Alina slept, her small breaths a soft rhythm against the night's hum, Liana found a worn notebook, its pages yellowed like the promises of their youth. She opened it, her pencil trembling, and began to write. Words spilled freely, a torrent of thoughts unchained—memories of her father's scars, the miniskirt's black stamp, the ash of burned books, now mingling with Guantánamo's dust, the warmth of Cuban smiles, the sting of Marko's distance. Each stroke was a liberation, her heart racing as the pages filled, the notebook a mirror to her soul. She wrote of Alina's laughter, a spark against the regime's gray, and of the market wives' whispers, their judgment a mirror to her personal shame. The notebook grew, a second one soon needed, its pages a vessel for her feelings—rage at the regime's lies, grief for her fractured marriage, hope for a future beyond the Iron Curtain's reach. Liana never felt more alive; the act of writing was a defiance, a spark that burned brighter than the Cuban sun, a vow to carve her own truth in a world that sought to silence her.

The notebook became Liana's sanctuary, its pages a rebellion against the silence stifling her Guantánamo shack. By lamplight, the bulb's flicker casting shadows on the worn concrete walls, her words wove a tapestry of resistance—memories of snow back home, dreams of freedom, and the children's hugs binding her to Cuba despite its chains. Marko's presence faded, his evenings lost to work's burdens, his distant gaze a fracture she couldn't bridge, leaving her heart raw. Yet the notebook steadied her, its ink a lifeline to the girl who'd defied policemen in her youth. She hid the pages under Alina's mattress, a secret as vital as the Western radio's static, a truth she'd carry to America, where freedom's light might shine. Her whisper—"courage, always"—echoed in her mind, fueling her vow to shield Alina from this dust-bound cage.

DECEPTIONS, THREATS, HYSTERIA

Liana and Marko were under constant surveillance from their own embassy and its puppets—strings yanked from Havana to their new home, a web they couldn't shake. Every word Liana and Marko breathed, every step they took was meticulously observed—recorded, stored in some gray folder, its leather creaking, for future use—a noose coiled tight around their necks, sweat beading on Liana's brow. Good thing technology was still a ghost then—crude, clunky—or Liana and Marko would've met a sharper, darker fate, a cell's cold slap or worse. The Communist Party of their country and its embassy had an invisible chokehold on them—exiles in foreign lands, no deviations from the scripted, sanctioned behavior allowed, a leash they felt in their bones, tugging on every whisper. One day, an embassy man rolled up to "check on" them—serious complaints, he said, his knock thudding on their thin door like a judge's gavel. He had that typical bureaucrat look—stubborn, his mind cemented in communist dogmas, his suit stiff as his creed, his pen tapping the folder with a dry tick. His eyes were vacant pools—no feeling, no compassion, and not a flicker of sympathy—just cold, hollow stares cutting through them, a machine in flesh. He opened his folder, pages crisp as ice, and read a list of petty bullet points—too small to stick, like dust motes swirling in the heat—but two hit as unreal, sharp as the wire they'd dodged, a jab she was still learning to parry.

The first was the baby goat. Liana and Marko had gotten it when they helped a Cuban man stranded on the road—miles from his shack, no electricity, no running water, just a big heart beating under his patched shirt, with sweat streaking his grin, and the Skoda's engine sputtering. He'd thrust the bleating animal into their Skoda, refusing Marko's pleas—"No, no, it's yours!"—a gift they couldn't dodge, his hands firm as he waved them off, dust gritty on Liana's hands. That goat became Alina's favorite pet—she fed it scraps from their stash, hauled green leaves from the yard, sometimes let it sleep in her room, its soft "baa" a lullaby she'd hum back, her blonde hair tangled as she nuzzled it. The neighborhood kids—five, six spilling in daily—loved it too, showering it with hugs, their laughter a chorus as it nuzzled hands. Alina giggling the loudest, her "Baa!" calls tugging leaves for the goat's nibble. It was heartwarming—those gap-toothed grins, Alina's nap with it curled by her side—soon it was a local star, folks knocking to ask if kids could play, a shy "Can we?" sung at their door. The little thing cried when Alina left it on the patio—big eyes wet, a bleat piercing until she came back to its side. Liana and Marko showed it to the embassy man—Alina holding its white fuzz high, beaming—no reaction, no twitch on his stone face, just a flip to the last, graver bullet point, his pen's tick a cold echo.

Marko designed new aqueducts in Guantánamo—new vital veins for a dying city—often trekking to the military zone near the U.S. Naval Base, wire glinting in the sun, dust and wire his backdrop, blueprints tucked under his arm, crinkling under his grip. The complaint demanded an investigation—of Marko, Liana, their whole family—suggesting they be shipped back home immediately, with no appeal, a sentence barked flat. Fear clawed

Liana—if that hit, their future, bleak as it was, would shatter, spilling ruin over Liana's mother, father, and every relative they'd left behind. Her father's camp scars—electric burns under his nails—were enough; Liana couldn't bear her mother's worried eyes searching for hers or her father's rasping cough growing worse because of them, their faces cracked open again by her misstep. That night, Liana and Marko whispered—like Liana's parents in the room she'd shared growing up—hushed, sharp, over the table, its wood cool under Liana's fingers, Alina's doll silent beside them, her small snores a shield they couldn't risk breaking, the night air thick with heat. They didn't know who listened—walls thin as paper, ears sharp as blades—didn't want Alina catching it; kids spill what they hear, and as Cuban people said, "There's always an eye to see you, an ear to hear you," a trap they'd learned young, a shadow they danced around.

Somehow, they dodged the storm—Marko's work too vital to the Cubans, Liana guessed, forcing the embassy to swallow its list, his base visits explained away with blueprints and a nod, his voice steady as he faced the man down. No pink slip, just more eyes, more ears, a tighter net on their little trio—Marko, Liana, Alina—watching every breath. They adapted—got used to the watch, the weight—treading light, a skill Liana would sharpen years later in their second Cuban plunge, a tale still brewing dark in her gut.

Days after the embassy man's visit, Liana noticed a shadow lingering near their shack, a figure in a white guayabera, his briefcase heavy, his eyes glinting under the shade of the palm fronds. The concrete path, gritty under her sandals, seemed to pulse with his presence, the humid air thick with menace. She froze, her Spanish whisper—"*Warning, danger*"—slipping out, a reflex from her Eastern European days when Party eyes trailed her every step. The figure stood by the guava tree she'd planted, its leaves trembling in the breeze, as if mocking her fragile hope. Liana's heart raced, memories of her father's camp scars surging, her resolve hardening.

She stepped closer, feigning calm, her voice steady in Spanish: "Who are you? What do you want?" The man's gaze darted, his footsteps crunching gravel as he slipped away, but the chill lingered. That night, Liana and Marko whispered over the worn table, Alina's doll resting nearby, her small snores a fragile shield. They spoke in hushed voices—"We need to be careful"—fearing the walls' thinness, the unseen ears sharper than the jets overhead. Liana's mind churned, the guayabera's shadow a noose tightening, a reminder of the embassy's lists, their lives cataloged like crimes. Her defiance flared, a spark from her youth's rebellion against policemen, now burning against Cuba's surveillance. She vowed to protect Alina, her heart a fortress against the regime's eyes, a truth she'd carry beyond this dust.

After those grossly unpleasant visits—the embassy and guayabera men's vacant stares like ghosts haunting Liana—days rolled on, with the same suffocating heat and humidity, temperatures stuck at 95 degrees, air thick as a wet rag over their faces, heavy with salt. Rain turned the city into a mud lake—people wading barefoot, clutching their shoes tightly; soles worn thin, slipping in the muck, one pair per coupon, as precious as breath. One day, Liana and Marko heard that the wife of a Cuban architect near them had cancer—whispers buzzing through the dust, the neighborhood a hive of worry. She was desperate, her two kids' faces her lifeline—eyes wide in the flickering lamplight, pain choking her at the thought of leaving them motherless, her voice breaking when she spoke their names. Local doctors shrugged, helpless, hands empty; she'd have to hit Havana, a road that loomed long. Her husband trekked weekends to hold her, his boots heavy with road dust, money draining fast, a strain bending his back until he cracked, his shoulders slumping under it. Then he came home, tears streaking his face, gaunt in the dawn's gray light—her discharge wasted by treatment, frail as a leaf, her steps a shuffle. Their block rallied—foreign families pooling meat, beef liver in packages—Alina clutching one, proud, tugging Liana's hand, her small fingers warm, "Mommy, she'll get better, right?" "Yes, sweetheart," Liana choked, her voice trembling with doubt—praying her husband would dodge the army's call, a shadow over frail hope, Liana's heart knotted tight as she squeezed Alina's fingers.

Every so often, their Cuban friends vanished—months gone, swallowed by silence, absence a hollow ache in their street. At first, Liana puzzled—then saw: military duty snatched them away, a claw from the dark. Liana couldn't stomach the endless exercises—hysteria she'd never dreamed of before Cuba—planes snarling low, engines a deafening growl, shaking the walls, sirens howling through the black, their wails piercing the humid night. Kids were taught to hate the U.S., to fear an invasion that never came, small voices chanting lies, words trembling in the school plazas. Gaslighting ran mad—power cut midmaneuvers, plunging them into dark, candles flickering with weak hope, jets rumbling, tearing the sky with a shriek, terror sown deep in fragile souls—Alina whimpering under her blanket, breath fast against the coarse fabric, friends' eyes wide in the gloom. Cubans shrugged off invasion scares—used to the noise, the game—but Alina and her playmates shook, fear clinging like damp heat, battered by hate drilled in, a cruel system stealing laughter, disastrous for any human, worse for them.

Friends stopped by—green uniforms, combat-ready—to kiss Liana and Marko goodbye, boots scuffing the dirt, a quick "Adios," Liana and Marko whispering "Good luck," a prayer for safe return, hands brushing in a fleeting grip. Months, years, sometimes—kids left behind, waiting by doors that didn't open, some never to return—war is cruel, good only for those playing politics with millions' lives, a game Liana would never grasp, her gut twisting at empty chairs, wives' quiet sobs.

Soon came the time to enroll Alina in first grade. She dove into classroom life, her eyes sparkling with joy, laughter ringing as she brought new friends home, their chatter filling their shack after school. It didn't last. One day, Liana and Marko were told Alina had been expelled—her crime: disrespecting the Revolution. They ran to the principal, Liana's sandals slapping the dusty path, to learn her sin. During a long speech in the school plaza, the sun scorching Alina's petite frame, she'd grown tired and sat on a José Martí monument. Liana's jaw dropped; she was hardly suppressing laughter at the absurd accusation. "She's six—she doesn't even know what the word revolution means, let alone understand your hour-long speeches in a language she is still learning!" Liana pleaded, the ridiculousness fueling her words, only digging a deeper hole. "And why build monuments a foot off the ground? She was exhausted!" Liana snapped, seeing horror in the principal's eyes, his face paling under the plaza's glare. She's done, Liana thought, school's over for her. Marko pulled strings, calling up some of Havana's big shots, voices crackling over the phone, who gave their unruly girl permission to return—on one condition: she'd steer clear of the memorial.

By the end of September, the Day of the Committees for the Defense of the Revolution loomed—a huge holiday, music pulsing like a heartbeat, festivities spilling, kids adorning building entrances with palm leaves, rustling in the breeze, cars with megaphones roaring Castro's "immense achievements," his party's triumph a lie louder than the hunger gnawing at bellies. Cubans had little to eat —crumbs, not feasts—but propaganda drowned the sad reality, a megaphone's bellow drowning empty plates. For Christmas, no one prepped—Christian holidays were banned, like back home—but Liana and Marko defied the dogmas, scrounging a tree, a pale echo of their country's pines, still perfect enough to brighten their days. Alina and Liana made paper ornaments—they colored them red and green, crayons scratching on rough paper. Soon the tree stood —a miracle for the neighborhood kids, glitter sparkling under the bulb's weak glow, gasps lighting their shack as they crowded round, eyes wide.

Soon after, they got blessed—or cursed—with another embassy visit, a "checkup" to ensure they stayed within permitted lines—Marko's work, Liana's silence, their lives. "What's this about Christmas?" the bureaucrat snapped, his icy face returned, breath sour with coffee, his inhumanly empty eyes narrowing. "Rumors you're unhappy with Cuba's conditions—why question the food for Cubans?" His voice rose, his finger jabbing the air, heavy with menace—they'd better obey, or else, his threat a lash. From those years, Liana learned that reprimanding with "return home" had two faces—for Marko and Liana, it was punishment for stepping out; for embassy rats, it meant tragedy, losing cars, dollars, and power clutched like gold. They survived that second visit—not knowing what lurked down the road, an unthinkable crime that'd rip a friend away, his blood a stain they'd face later.

Before leaving, the bureaucrat warned them—a new engineer, transferred from Havana to Guantánamo, unruly, unpredictable, but damn good at his job, sent here as punishment. "Watch him closely," he hissed, "any deviation, call us—don't you dare befriend him, he's marked." Days later, he came—full of life and laughter, tall and handsome, loud-talking, fast-walking, boots thumping the floor, "Hola!" booming as he swept in, making friends with everybody, playing with Alina, her "uncle" in a heartbeat, loving all, winning hearts with a grin that cracked the gray, dust swirling in his wake. Liana and Marko loved him as a brother—weekends laughing, his voice a roar over their table—never once thinking to call the embassy, his mark be damned. He was a dear friend they cherished dearly, a light they held tight.

One evening, Liana and Marko hosted a meal, their shack alive with Cuban neighbors, the new engineer's laughter booming like a drum. The worn table groaned under the shared rice and beans, the air thick with the sweet scent of plantains and barbecued meat, a rare feast in Guantánamo's scarcity. The engineer, exiled from Havana for his free tongue, spun tales of salsa-filled nights, his

"¡Hola!" a spark that lit the room, Alina giggling as he tossed her in the air, her doll forgotten on the floor. Liana's Spanish flowed—"*Amigos, bienvenidos*"—mixing with rapid Cuban dialects, their laughter a bridge over the language gap. Rosa, from their first day, squeezed Liana's hand, her stories of her children blending with Liana's memories of snow. The warmth cut through the regime's shadow, their bond a defiance against the embassy's eyes. Liana's heart swelled; the community was a lifeline, yet Marko's quiet nods, his mind on work, hinted at the fracture growing between them, a pang she pushed aside for the night's joy.

They had no idea that not long after, they would bow their heads in memory of this extraordinary man—his life cut short, taken from them, from everyone who loved him—hoping whoever snuffed him out faced harsh justice, a prayer whispered into the void he left behind.

THE EPIDEMIC

Liana had heard plenty about the successes of Cuban medicine—praises sung loud in papers back home, a chorus of "miracles"—but she had no opinion, just a shrug, until one night a hurricane screamed over their heads, a beast that tore her doubts to ribbons. No advice, no warning—just a neighbor's shout, "*¡Cuidado!*" swallowed by the dark as howling winds slammed Guantánamo, palms bending low, fighting to stand, their fronds whipping like flags in surrender, a crack splitting one's trunk as it fell. Flying debris battered their walls—shingles, planks, a tin can clanging against the door, and a shutter groaning loose—tornadoes swirled mercilessly, a roar drowning all thought, the noise a claw in Liana's ears, deafening thunder, splitting the sky with white-hot knives that lit up the chaos. Lights blinked powerlessly—flicker, flicker—then died, plunging Marko, Alina, and Liana into darkness for days, a void thick with dread, the air heavy with what was to come. It wasn't rain—the heavens ripped open, dumping millions of gallons, a deluge that turned streets into quick-moving rivers of mud, storm drains a fantasy of some far-off future, a pipe dream for fools. For the first time, Liana saw earth and sky fuse—a monolithic wall, life and breath crushed under nature's wrath, a fist no human could dodge, no prayer could turn, its weight a warning of worse to come.

The water rose fast—ankles, knees, in a cold grip climbing—and before Marko, Alina, and Liana could blink, rats invaded their home, scrambling for shelter, their claws scratching wood, their tails flicking through the murk, a squeak piercing the dark. They screamed in horror—high, wild shrieks—jumping onto beds, mattresses creaking under them, with no refuge as the flood chased them higher up, its stink a slap. Water poured in, brown and foul, reeking of rot, filling every inch, and sloshing straw furniture—their table, a chair—floating like wreckage in a dead sea. There, between the squeak of rats and the tide's lap, they spent the night—Alina crying "Mami!" clinging to Liana's neck, her sodden doll pressed tight to her chest, Marko's arm a brace, his jaw tight as he growled, "Hold her, don't let go." Morning broke—the sky sparkling blue, birds back with angelic chirps, a cruel concert over the ruin, as if to mock the calamities clawing lives apart, their song sharp against their sodden clothes, their trembling hands.

Palm trees lay snapped in the mud, roots torn free, surrounded by debris—splinters, metal, rags ripped from balconies, laundry that Cubans chased desperately through the mire, their shouts a chorus of need—shirts, skirts, all rationed, one per coupon, too precious to lose. Who'd let their kids' uniforms vanish, swept off in the flood's greed? Marko waded out, boots squelching, helping a neighbor snag a shirt from the muck, his grunt a shared ache, his hands slick with effort, mud caking his fingers. The water came browner than ever—swamp-thick, stinking of decay—they had gas to boil it, a rare luck most Cubans didn't have, their pots cold, electricity off for days, wires dangling dead like broken veins. Their clothes turned dark gray, clinging to them like a weight of shame. Liana showered with her mouth shut. "Don't open your mouth, don't speak, sweetheart," she begged Alina, her heart a ball of worries, Alina's small hand trembling in hers as water stung her eyes, her cough spiking Liana's dread each time it rasped. Soon, kids sickened worse—their bellies bloated, parasites thriving in the filth, mosquitoes swarming, their buzz a taunt in the haze that choked the air. Then they learned an epidemic of meningitis was sweeping through—a word that froze Liana's blood, a blade at her throat, a terror sharper than the storm's roar. A Cuban friend's son had caught it years back—complications left him barely walking, talking, his brain damaged with no hope to mend, his mother's eyes hollow as graves when she said his name, her voice a ghost trailing off.

Fear enveloped every family with kids—Liana's worst of all, Alina's cough a dagger each night, her blonde curls damp with what Liana prayed was heat, not fever. Tragedy struck—a friend's toddler son perished, meningitis snatching his breath, his tiny shoes empty by their door, his mother's wail a wound Liana couldn't unhear, a sound that clawed her sleep. Liana was terrified, praying to God to spare Alina, her little sweetheart, her hair a flicker in the dark, praying for her friends too, their laughter dimmed to whimpers in the haze. There was this girl—three, maybe four—the sweetest child, with chocolate skin, curly hair spilling down her back, always barefoot, her toes caked with earth. She half-lived at their home, slipping in at dawn, her hungry eyes—dark, wide—waiting for Liana to make breakfast, a fresco's cool fizz a treat she'd sip slow, her giggle a "Gracias, Mami!" as her soft hands brushed Liana's, her kisses a heaven's gift on Liana's cheek. She'd stay all day, Alina and her weaving games—tag, dolls, a chase sparking laughs that rang like sunshine—her cheer a balm to Liana's heart, a chorus cutting Guantánamo's gray. Years later, she's likely a mother—wherever she is, Liana hopes she knows that she loved her like her own, misses her even now, her memory an ache that slices sharp. When they said goodbye, her hug was the strongest—her small arms fierce, refusing to let go, crying, "Stay, Mami!"—and Liana learned that hearts break for real, a pain that cuts even today, her voice a scar Liana carries deep, a wound that whispers her name.

Worried sick about the epidemic, a Cuban friend gave Liana and Marko a pediatrician's name—the best in the city, a miracle man, she swore, her voice calm with trust that steadied Liana. Marko and Liana drove to his house—an old Spanish gem, with heavy wooden doors swinging to a garden shaded by flamboyant trees, their red blooms hiding forgotten architecture, a jewel glinting in the haze. Despite the heat, it was cool inside—high ceilings lifting the air, ceramic mosaic floors swirling color, old furniture carved with care, worn but proud, whispering stories of better days. The door opened, and Liana met him—not tall, his eyes smiling behind glasses, his clothes simple, a worn shirt loose on his frame. With time, Liana would learn he was a man of great character—noble, modest, revered in Cuba's medical world—but above all, his heart beat gold under that frayed cloth, a pulse of care that held them up like a root in a storm. He expected them—his wife, three sons, their smiles warm, a nod from the eldest catching Liana's eye—yet exhaustion clung to him, etched deep from grueling days and nights at the hospital, battling the epidemic's claw. Liana spilled her fears—Alina, her cough, the meningitis shadow—and with his soft voice, his mild manners, he breathed calm into her, a steady hand on her storm, his gentle "She'll be fine," a lifeline Liana grabbed tight. He'd visit tomorrow, he said, and they left—Marko's grip on the wheel looser, Liana's breath easier—a flicker of hope piercing the haze like a star through fog.

The next day, Marko brought him home with his youngest son —a lanky boy, shy, trailing his dad, his nod quiet but kind. They spoke, laughed, and Liana's worries washed away, a tide pulling back under his steady gaze. There was something in him—faith in God, in people—a strange, solid reassurance, like a root under Liana's feet, grounding her fear. He checked Alina, prescribed medicine, his hands gentle on her brow as she squirmed, her giggle breaking his focus with a smile. When Liana offered snacks—bread, cheese, and a thin slice—he declined, polite, his "No, gracias" soft, but his eyes, his son's, spoke differently. Liana froze, astonished—their hunger peeked through, a shadow they tried to hide, a pang that hit her deep, twisting like a knife. Here was one of Cuba's best pediatricians, hours of fighting a horrifying epidemic, and he was hungry—exhausted and hungry, his son's thin frame a silent echo, their smiles brave but frail, a mirror to the want they'd fled back home. Like her own country, Cuba had skilled doctors but little else —no technology, medicine scarce as rain, and hands tied by a system's rot. Years later, Liana would see it raw—Marko's hernia operation, a grim tale of rust and haste, a scalpel's edge too dull—but then, it was this man's eyes that cut her, their want a wound she couldn't unsee.

One sweltering afternoon, illness gripped Liana, a fever burning through her bones, her body aching as if the Cuban sun had seared her from within. The shack's concrete floor, cool and unyielding under her bare feet, echoed with the doctor's footsteps as he arrived, his worn bag clinking with sparse tools, his eyes soft with concern. "Lie down, Liana," he said, his voice low, steady, the air thick with antiseptic and the rustle of palm fronds outside. She obeyed, sinking onto the sagging mattress—a frail refuge—breath shallow. Trembling, she lifted the hem of her blouse just enough to bare the flushed skin above her heart. He laid his palm there—clinical, yet impossibly tender—fingers resting over the wild racing of her pulse. Liana froze. A sudden tide of vulnerability and desire surged through her exhausted body, an ache for the affection that had withered in Marko's silence, for the simple warmth of a man's touch.

The moment hung heavy, the shack's humid air a weight between them. Liana's eyes met the doctor's and locked—his smitten spark now a quiet, steady flame, her heart trembling with a forbidden pull. Weak from fever and from the sudden surge of longing, she felt the girl she used to be stir inside her. Then shame coiled sharp in her chest—Marko, distant, yet still her husband, and Alina, sleeping in the next room, anchored her to duty. "I'm fine," she whispered, voice barely a breath. She sat up, tugging her blouse back into place. The spell broke like a wave pulling back from shore. The doctor nodded at once. His hand lifted away, slow and respectful, his eyes gentle with unspoken understanding. No words were needed; the silent promise was clear: he would never cross the line she had just drawn.

Liana's fever broke that night, but the encounter lingered, a secret she tucked into her notebook, its pages now a haven for truths she couldn't speak. She wrote of the doctor's kindness, his hands a contrast to the cruelty surrounding him in the hospital nightmare, his affection a light against the grayness that choked her marriage. The words spilled freely, her pencil scratching under the lamplight, capturing the ache of her heart—torn between loyalty to Marko and the pull of a connection that felt like freedom. She remembered the miniskirt's black stamp, the ash of burned books, and saw in the doctor a kindred spirit, his defiance hidden in his care for Guantánamo's children, a spark she'd carry into her manuscript. The notebook grew, its pages a rebellion against the silence, a vow to protect Alina and honor the truths that bound her to this island, its people, and the doctor's quiet flame.

A few days later, Liana made sandwiches—cheese, bread, a thin smear of salami—and took them to the hospital where the doctor worked, seventy-two hours straight, a warrior in the dark, his steps heavy but sure. Liana wanted to thank him, to beg him back to their shack, her sandals quick with gratitude on the cracked path. The hospital reeked—of poverty stark, no machines humming, just beds and moans, scant tools for a war against death's grip. At the "Intensive Care" door, Liana knocked, her voice shaking, asking for him. He came out—his face gray from sleepless nights, desperation cracking his calm—and nearly screamed, "Don't enter, it's dangerous!" Liana froze, but saw them—kids convulsing, vomiting, a boy stumbling, dizzy, calling "Mami!" on tiny feet, his voice a knife twisting Liana's gut. She can't erase it—beds of writhing pain, a hell she fled, her sandals slapping the floor in retreat, her breath a sob. How many survived, how many scarred by the claws of meningitis? Liana didn't know—just fear and indignation, a tsunami rising in her.

In several months, the meningitis epidemic grew exponentially, while continuing to be hidden from public knowledge; it lasted five endless months—children died, others suffered irreversible brain damage, while still battling asthma and parasites, their frail bodies crumbling under the weight. This was a country—its leaders keeping millions in poverty's chokehold, no food grown, no clean water for its poorest towns, kids malnourished, their frail frames too weak to fight disease, bellies swollen with want, a scream louder than any storm's roar. Heartbreaking—and for the millionth time, Liana asked: Why no mass rebellion? A question she still can't answer, a weight she carries, heavy as the mud they'd waded through.

As the epidemic raged, the doctor's exhaustion deepened, his visits to their shack a lifeline Liana clung to, his bag clinking with sparse tools, his eyes hollow from sleepless nights. He came unannounced, his boots dusty from the hospital path, his face lined with the weight of lost children, yet his smile for Alina a spark in the gloom. "How's the little one?" he'd ask, his voice hoarse, his hands gentle as he checked her brow, his fear for her well-being a silent undercurrent. Liana offered him a seat on the worn stool, a cup of boiled water, her Spanish steady as she spoke of Alina's play, but his gaze lingered on her, his concern for Liana's weariness a quiet affection she felt in her bones. "You need rest too," he said, his voice low, honoring the boundaries she held, his respect for her marriage a wall he wouldn't cross. Liana's heart stirred, the pull of his care a tide against Marko's absence, but she remained faithful, her vows an anchor. He left, promising to return, his exhaustion a burden she wished to share, a bond forged in Cuba's trials.

Summer brought heat—suffocating, worse than the storm's wet lash—dust everywhere, settling on furniture the second Liana wiped it, a gritty haze dancing in crazy streams when wind kicked up, sending kids and parents to hospitals, asthma choking their breaths, their wheezes a chorus piercing the night. Water stayed chocolate-brown—showering … Liana wondered if she was cleaner or filthier, her skin itching with doubt, a question with no end. "Keep your mouth closed, sweetheart," Liana told Alina during baths, no easy task for her busy imagination, her chatter bubbling despite Liana's pleas, her "But why, Mami?" a spark Liana couldn't hush, though fear tried to douse it. Diarrhea hit everywhere—parasites in every kid Liana knew, their swollen bellies screaming malnutrition, protein a ghost they chased, their eyes dull with a hunger Liana couldn't fill. Even now, Liana can't grasp how Cuba's communist leaders let children rot—for a revolution's "glory," empty words, hollow lies piling like dust on a grave. Liana tried—fed Alina's friends, their friends, every scrap they had, cheese sliced thin as paper, bread torn small—but it was a drop in an ocean of suffering, a country drowning under its own weight, its leaders blind to the wails. So Liana continued her notes—her Cuban manuscript, a ledger of thoughts scratched in the dark from Guantánamo's days, the pen's scrape a vow to hold her resolve. She etched what her eyes saw—mud, moans, and hunger—what her ears heard—wails, coughs, and silences—so she'd never forget, so no one should, a record to stand against time. The young must know what their parents endured, what Alina's friends bore, the weight of a system that crushed their laughter, their frail bodies breaking under the grip of scarcity. It was a debt Liana owed their kids—Alina, her friends, all who came after—a vow she sealed in ink, her hand steady despite the haze, her heart fierce for their future, a truth to break the chains of silence.

DOLLAR'S REIN, CUBA'S PAIN

There were two classes in Liana's country: Communist Party members, cloaked in power, and everyone else, struggling to survive in their shadow. In Cuba, two more classes carved the divide: those paid in U.S. dollars, kings of a broken land, and those—like Marko—handed the "*peso rojo*," a convertible tender for communist comrades, as limp as the system it propped up. The dollar was Cuba's ruler, pulsing through the black market's veins, the failing economy's cruel master—a king in every Cuban's dreams, a glint they chased through storm and dread. Liana knew little of its reign until they visited Cubalse, the dollar store in Santiago de Cuba—an unforgettable day, marked by an earthquake's jolt that shook the floor, a tremor Liana felt in her gut. She'd feared quakes to panic mode—heart racing, breath gone—but that day, she brushed it aside, stepping into the store, Alina's hand warm in hers, her eyes wide at the glow.

Everything was there—food stacked high, clothes in colors they'd forgotten, shoes sturdy enough to last—abundance overwhelming, a slap against the "nothing" of local shops, their frog-green, yellowed, sagging floaties a nightmare Liana couldn't shake from Havana. The aisles stretched endlessly: canned milk towered in pyramids, chocolate bars were wrapped in silver foil, jars of peanut butter gleamed under fluorescent lights, bags of rice sat in twenty-kilo sacks, cooking oil came in plastic bottles, and even breakfast cereals featured cartoon mascots smiling from colorful boxes. The clothing racks overflowed—dresses in floral prints, jeans with metal rivets, T-shirts with logos of American bands, sneakers with cushioned soles, and even winter coats lined with synthetic fur. Liana ran her fingers over a pair of sandals in Alina's size, the leather soft, the straps adjustable—things she'd never seen in Guantánamo's markets.

Alina ran through the aisles, her blonde curls bouncing, eyeing toys they couldn't buy with their peso rojo. Her "Mommy, please!" was a tug Liana couldn't answer. Liana asked a saleswoman—pointing to a desk with guayaberas, those cursed floaties—"Is that all?" her voice sharp, her Spanish proficiency clear despite the Cuban dialect's rush. The saleswoman's look was cold, total disregard—as if their lack of dollars dumped them in the murky pile of the insignificant, a class below her sneer. Rage flared—discrimination by tender was the last straw in Cuba's dust, a betrayal of the "comrades" lie. With Alina whining for a doll they couldn't afford, Liana knelt, pointing to the barefoot kids outside—their hungry eyes glinting, their hands outstretched. "See them, sweetheart?" Liana said, her throat tight, teaching Alina a lesson no child should learn, her frown a mirror to Liana's shame.

Years later, they'd taste that sting again—returning home, their Soviet plane broke down, stranding them in Brussels overnight. Border police took their passports, and when the time came to return them, a uniformed man—spotting their country's stamp—threw them to the floor, a deliberate arc to humiliate, marking them third-class, worthy only of disrespect. A storm of rage exploded in Liana—she barked, "Pick up the passports and hand them to us!" in Spanish, as clear as glass. He froze, colleagues and passengers staring, then picked them up, handed them over with a muttered excuse, his eyes dodging Liana's. Marko's nod—quiet, proud—said enough; Alina clutched her doll tighter, sensing something bigger than her years could name.

Desperate for essentials, Liana ventured into the black market, a shadowy corner of Guantánamo where dollars ruled and whispers carried risk. The air was thick with sweat and secrecy, a stall tucked behind a crumbling wall, its vendor's eyes darting like the rats in their flood-soaked shack. Liana's Spanish, steady now, bartered for soap and shampoo, "How much for this?" Her voice was low, her peso rojo clutched tight. The vendor demanded dollars, his sneer a mirror to the Cubalse saleswoman's, and Liana's heart raced—each transaction a dance with danger, with the Secret Service's eyes never far away. But after a moment's hesitation, he snatched the peso rojo, muttering, "Fine, take it," a small victory in the underbelly. Liana's hands trembled as she tucked the bag away, the soap's weight a fragile triumph. The moral toll hit hard—her defiance, forged in Eastern European resistance, clashed with the shame of providing for her family through Cuba's shadows. "For Alina," she whispered, her resolve a spark against the regime's shadow, but the weight of complicity lingered, a ghost in the scarcity. The vendor's glance darted to a guayabera-clad figure nearby, his briefcase heavy, a reminder of the eyes that never slept, tightening the noose around her heart.

Hunger and want fueled prostitution's bloom—staggering to see young girls, some barely teens, knocking door to door, hoping that a lone foreign specialist might trade. A pair of pantyhose, a blouse, makeup—any chip to bargain. One day, as Liana cooked lunch for Alina's playmates, two beautiful girls knocked—their eyes down, not expecting Liana, a woman, at home. They turned to leave, but Liana called, "Come in!" They talked long—their voices soft, sharing how hard it was to find clothes, to feel pretty. "Why sell yourself for a rag?" Liana asked, her heart sinking. "You're beautiful, no matter what—don't break what can't be fixed." They were hungry, desperate—Liana's words didn't stick, their steps heavy as they left. Liana didn't think the government sanctioned it—more, it was encouraged, a pipeline for police to glean secrets from foreigners, a trap woven tight.

Days rolled on—meningitis raging, dust cloaking their lives, and water murky as lies. Their Cuban friends—Marko's coworkers, the doctor—were the only light, their warmth a fire against the gray. Talking with the doctor was a treat—knowledgeable, informed, they'd lose nights to politics, culture, and Cuba's cracks—his modesty a quiet strength. One day, burned out from the hospital, he asked for a sandwich—his hunger raw, unhidden. The bread and salami vanished fast; Liana offered another, his "No, no" fading as it disappeared, his eyes grateful, the second gone before she blinked. Exhaustion had carved deep lines in his face, his hands trembling from endless shifts, yet his smile for Alina remained gentle, his care a steady light through the epidemic's darkness. "You will save them all," Liana said, her voice thick. He shook his head: "I try—for her, for all of them." His words hung heavy, a shared burden binding them closer, his quiet flame flickering against Marko's growing distance.

Liana and her neighbors organized a small fiesta for the children, a defiance against the grip of poverty. Their stoop became a stage, Rosa bringing a worn drum, its beat echoing conga rhythms, kids dancing, their laughter a spark no scarcity could snuff. Liana's voice rang clear, Spanish steady as she handed out sandwiches and fresco, Alina twirling with friends, her doll resting on the ground—forgotten in the joy. The Cuban architect, his laughter dimmed by his wife's illness, joined with a sack of plantains, his "For the kids" a quiet vow. Their makeshift celebration—colors, shouts, and joy—cut through the haze, a rebellion against the neglect surrounding them. Liana's heart filled with happiness, the community a lifeline, yet Marko's quiet nods, his mind on work, deepened the fracture she couldn't bridge, a pang she buried in the music's pulse.

Soon after, Carnival erupted in Guantánamo's dusty streets—a kaleidoscope of colors bursting through the weight of crushing poverty, a defiant pulse against destiny's iron grip. Kids banged metal cans as drums, their makeshift rhythms weaving with conga beats that pulled feet to dance, faces lit up with a spark that no poverty could douse. The air thrummed with life—sweat, the tang of beer, and the hum of voices rising above the heat. Liana stood at the edge of the crowd, her heart lifting as Alina twirled, her blonde curls bouncing, her giggle a bright thread in the music's weave. The neighborhood, usually choked by dust and want, transformed into a stage of defiance, palm fronds strung across shacks, their rustle a soft counterpoint to the roar of the drums. Liana's eyes traced the crowd—Cubans, poor and crushed, their fire unyielding, a shield against despair. Marko's arm brushed hers, a rare ease, making her heart beat faster, a fragile hope.

Kids darted through the crowd, their bare feet kicking up the ground, their laughter a defiance echoing the hostilities they endured—hunger, surveillance, and illnesses. A girl, her curly hair spilling down her back, tugged Alina's hand, their chase sparking giggles that rang over the din, a balm to Liana's heart. She thought of the Cubalse store, the barefoot children outside, their hungry eyes pleading for bubble gum, and her rage flared anew at the system that crushed them. Yet here, in the carnival's heat, they danced, their joy a spark that no poverty could shutter. Liana joined the sway, her sandals scuffing the cracked path, her voice rising with the crowd's, "Keep dancing!" her Spanish steady, a call to hold fast against the gray.

The night deepened, filled with endless hugs and smiles in the heat's pulse, the crowd's roar a singular force, exceeding any dream Liana had known in her Eastern European cage. Beer bottles clinked, their tang sharp against the haze, love's hum weaving through the chaos. Liana's thoughts drifted to her past—her father's scars, the miniskirt's stamp—and her resolve hardened, a vow to protect Alina, to carry this fire to a freer land. Alina spun closer, her giggle lost in the beat, her small hand finding Liana's, a tether to hope. Marko's nod, quiet but warm, held a fleeting connection, a moment Liana clutched tight, knowing it might fade. The carnival's spark burned bright, a testament to a people who danced through pain, their strength a lesson that Liana would carry beyond Cuba.

Marko's big project neared completion, Guantánamo bracing for Castro's July 26th celebration. Work ran 24/7, people drained, yet the next day it closed—for repairs, a farce. Roads stayed broken, asphalt a myth, no water station to curb the endless ills—nothing trumped the façade, a "blooming" society fighting "imperialist demons," lies thick as mud. The MIGs cut the sky with raging thunder. Police were everywhere, and men in white guayaberas, their faces solemn and expressionless, invaded the city, with fear rampant. The day of the inauguration, the promised bus to the plaza never came; instead, their neighborhood—foreign engineers, specialists—was cordoned off, Secret Service swarming, locking them in, kids barred from play, a war zone's hum. Marko couldn't see his project unveiled, a sting he swallowed silently, his jaw set as they stayed locked inside.

Fed up—surveillance, lies choking them—Liana, Marko, and Alina fled one weekend to a hidden beach few knew of, far from eyes. Sierra Cristal's mountains rose on one side, black shell-strewn sand sparkled on the other—a paradise, palms tall, murmuring in the heat. The ocean gleamed unreal blue, transparent, waves soft as a sigh. They lingered, serenity strange—Alina splashing, Marko's laugh free.

As they left, late afternoon, a woman threw herself at their Skoda, clutching a baby girl, screaming, "Take her!"—trying to shove her through the window. They froze. She wore rags—a threadbare dress torn at the hem, barefoot in the sand, her dark hair matted with sweat. Her little cabin stood yards away, a fragile shelter of branches lashed together with vines, roofed with dried palm leaves that rattled in the breeze. No walls, just gaps where wind whistled through. No water, no electricity—the Revolution's promises empty in this forgotten corner.

Four of her children stood outside the shack, naked and barefoot, thin bodies streaked with dirt, bellies swollen from malnutrition, ribs stark under taut skin. The oldest, maybe seven, clutched a stick, eyes hollow; the next, a girl of five, swayed on stick-thin legs; twins, three years old, sat on the ground, their distended stomachs round against skeletal frames, flies buzzing around running noses. They stared, silent, as their mother thrust the baby at Liana—six months old, wrapped in a scrap of sheet, her tiny face flushed, and eyes wide with hunger.

"No life here," the woman sobbed, tears cutting tracks through dust-caked cheeks, "no water, no power, no future. Take her—give her milk, clothes, a chance." Her voice broke, her hands trembling as she pushed the baby closer. Marko gripped the wheel, his voice low, "We can't." Alina cried from the back, "I want a sister!"—her wail a knife through Liana's heart. The woman's eyes locked on Liana's, with a desperate, "Please. She's starving. I have nothing."

Liana took the baby, her weight feather-light, her skin hot with fever, her tiny fists clenched against the rags. The infant's eyes searched hers, trusting, innocent—a life already broken before it even began. Liana's throat closed, tears blurring the four siblings standing silent, their swollen bellies an eloquent accusation. The cabin's palm roof sagged, branches splintered, a home no child deserved. "How do you survive?" Liana whispered. The woman laughed, bitter, "We don't. We dig for water with bare hands, dwell in darkness for nights, and eat hunger for breakfast."

Marko spoke reason, his voice thick, "We'll bring food tomorrow." The woman shook her head, "Too late for promises." It took minutes to calm Alina's sobs, to return the baby—her weight a terrifying truth in Liana's arms. The woman clutched her daughter close, whispering "Perdóname," as they drove away. Silence rode home, Alina's sniffles soft, Liana's heart shattered. That cabin, those children, that mother's cry—if poverty had a face, it lived there, branches and palm leaves the only separation between life and despair.

GUANTÁNAMO'S BLOOD AND BONDS

Marko's contract was fading, Guantánamo's end closing in. A strange nostalgia curled sharply in Liana's chest. She ached for her mother's soft hum, her father's gaze scarred from the camps, but she'd miss their friends here: the brash engineer, his laugh a spark; the doctor, their lifeline with steady hands; the kids streaming through their home, Alina's sisters and brothers in rain and sun, their giggles echoing in the warm dusk. As Marko's work dwindled, Liana craved home. Then Liana's mother arrived, a burst of light. She fell for Cuba—its pulsing heat, palm fronds whispering in the heat, her eyes bright. She loved the engineer's brass, his tales pulling cackles till tears spilled, and revered the doctor, his care a marvel she'd whisper, her voice warm. The kids swarmed her. With no Spanish in her mouth, they still loved her, giggling at her waving hands, hugging her knees, claiming her as abuela in chatter needing no words, like Alina's games in their weathered shack.

Illness hit them hard, once again. Liana's mother's cough tore her chest, fever clouding her eyes. An amoeba churned Liana's insides, fever scorching her skin, her legs collapsing like cotton.

Marko rushed them to the emergency room, but chaos greeted them—no medicine, doctors shrugging, and beds creaking with moans like plague nights. They turned them away, Liana's mother's breath a faint rasp, Liana's head spinning like a storm. Their friend, the doctor, came. Medicine heavy in his bag, he checked them with soft hands. His "You'll mend" pulled them through where the hospital crumbled. Liana's fever broke, Alina's grandma's cough quieted, and her visit ended with kids waving, their hugs a gift she carried home.

Still, there were moments of sheer happiness—when a child of a foreign specialist recovered from a terrifying burn. The kid was playing at home, walking backward, when he tripped—falling onto a white-hot frying pan his mother had set on the ground to cool. His little legs, wrapped in leaking bandages, ached, hurting as he cried hysterically, his parents desperate, their faces pale with worry. One Sunday, they drove to the beach, waves whispering against the shore, the Caribbean's gentle caress soothing his wounds. All day, he played in the water, the sand soft under his feet, forgetting the pain, free of it at last. That night, his mother came, happy tears streaming down her face, clutching him close. A miracle happened—the wounds, cleansed, revealed healing skin, pink and tender. The neighborhood erupted in celebration, laughter ringing through the humid air, hugging the boy and covering him with joyful kisses.

Alina glowed—skin golden, hair blonder, her Spanish sharp with slang that Liana and Marko tried to curb, her laughter bright as the tropical sun. She belonged. While her school scores soared, her rebellion flared—she refused to leave, her friends being her world. She loved the engineer, exiled for speaking freely, calling him "uncle," giggling as he swung her on his back, his hands steady, their bond a light.

Alina's love for the engineer, her "uncle," was a spark that lit their shack, his booming laugh a defiance of Guantánamo's bleak everyday life. Exiled from Havana for his free tongue, he carried a fire that warmed their days, his stories a rebellion against the regime's silence. One weekend, under a sky blazing with tropical heat, he swept into their home, his boots thumping the floor, a sack of plantains slung over his shoulder like a trophy. "Let's feast!" he roared, his grin wide as the Caribbean, and Liana laughed, her heart lifting despite the unseen eyes trailing their steps. Marko uncorked a bottle of rum, its amber glow a rare treasure, and they gathered around the table, Alina perched on the engineer's knee, her laughter echoing as he spun tales of Havana's nightlife, its salsa pulsing through forbidden clubs, the rhythm a heartbeat against Castro's decrees.

The afternoon stretched, the rum's warmth loosening their tongues, the shack's walls humming with life. The engineer taught Alina a Cuban song, his voice deep and off-key, her small hands clapping to the beat, her Spanish slang sharp with delight. "Tío, again!" she squealed, her blonde curls bouncing, and he obliged, his eyes twinkling with a mischief that reminded Liana of her father's defiance, his whispered truths in their modest flat. They danced, the engineer swinging Alina in circles, her laughter a burst of light in the humid air, the plantains frying in a pan, their sweet scent mingling with the sea's salt. Liana shared stories of her youth—the miniskirt stamped black, the ash of burned books—and the engineer nodded, his hand steady on her shoulder, his "You're a fighter, Liana" a balm to her doubts. Marko, usually quiet, joined in, recounting his blueprints for Guantánamo's aqueducts, their lines a hope to mend a broken city, though the regime's neglect mocked his work.

As dusk fell, the engineer led them to the guava tree Liana had hacked from the dust, its branches heavy with fruit, a triumph over the barren soil. Alina climbed its boughs, her hands sticky with juice, the engineer catching her as she leaped, his laughter a roar that drowned the distant jets. They sat under the tree, the stars piercing the haze, sharing plantains and rum, their voices weaving a tapestry of defiance— he told Alina a silly story about a fish who could talk, and she listened, her eyes wide open, her hand resting in his, and there was a bond between them, filling Liana's heart with love and tenderness.

That night, as Alina slept, her doll nestled close, Liana and Marko sat with the engineer on the patio, the air thick with heat and memory. The engineer spoke of his exile, his voice low, the regime's punishment for his loud truths a wound he wore like a badge. "They can't silence us all," he said, his eyes glinting, and Liana felt a fire kindle, her Cuban manuscript a vow to carry his spark.

His laughter, his songs, were a light against Guantánamo's gray, but the regime's eyes loomed, their shadow a threat that Liana couldn't shake. Days later, his blood would stain the morgue, his songs silenced, but that weekend, under the guava tree's murmur, they were alive, their bond a fire that no knife could snuff.

Plane tickets home lagged, delays piling up with no reason given, each empty mailbox a stab of frustration. Liana's parents, anxious, sent letters begging them to come back, their familiar handwriting smudged by the humid air, their pleas both comforting and cutting. Guantánamo's mail carried comfort and dread—letters from Liana's parents, sliced open by unseen eyes, their torn edges rough under her fingers, stamped "Received in damaged condition." They knew—everyone did—their words, like those of other specialists, were read by shadows, a trap like embassy lists. That day, Liana grabbed the mail, her heart lifting at her mother's handwriting, the paper's faint ink scent pulling her home, and she stopped by the engineer's apartment. He flung the door open—fresh from a shower, towel round his waist, with another on his head, singing a Cuban tune, his voice booming, happy. He tossed Alina a wink as they dropped his letters, his grin wide through the wooden blinds' sun, warming the dusty air. Hours later, horror crashed in.

Late evening, Alina close to sleep, her doll nestled close by, when a compatriot burst in. No knock, the door slamming, car horns blaring outside, he trembled, his voice cracking. "They hurt him, hospital!" he screamed. They scrambled—"Who?"—until his name hit: their engineer, knifed, his life fading, his song dead. Alina leaped, sobbing, "Uncle!" Her cry cut like a blade where his wink had glowed. Marko bolted for the hospital, his boots kicking dust. Liana gripped Alina's hand, whispering, "He'll be okay," the lies choking her as Alina shook. Cars screeched. Three State Security men, uniforms crisp, their faces marble-cold, stepped in. "Where's your husband?" one barked. "Hospital—we heard," Liana stammered, Alina heavy, tears soaking her. "Your friend's in the morgue," he said, his eyes flat. Alina's wails pierced the air—she knew, with her child's instinct, drowning in sobs.

The world spun. Liana cried, Alina cried, the night endless, swallowing hope. Liana stayed beside Alina, hugging and kissing her face till dawn, her damp hair clinging to Liana's cheek, her whimpers fading to sleep. Morning brought Marko home, his eyes hollow. For the first time, Liana saw him cry, his sobs raw in the stifling air. Liana clung to him, terrorized, listening as he described the morgue. Their friend lay there, a huge wound on his chest, with blood's metallic tang heavy in the room. The murderer's knife had plunged into his heart, pierced his lungs, and reached his liver. He tried to flee, stumbling, his palms leaving bloody marks on the walls, their smears stark against chipped paint, a sign of his lost fight. It was too late—he died in the hospital, his breath gone, his sunshine smile and songs a ghost now. They called the embassy daily—no one came, their silence a cold slap. Defenseless, abandoned, they felt powerless. Rumors swirled in the city, whispers hissing through dusty streets. Two days later, Liana spotted men in white guayaberas with heavy black briefcases, sneaking into the empty house next door, their footsteps crunching on gravel. Playing dumb, Liana confronted them: "What are you doing here?

Someone was just murdered!" They looked unpleasantly surprised and left, but that night, sleepless, Liana saw a figure in the garden, two eyes peering through their blinds as they slept, their gaze chilling her skin. Fear was choking Liana, doom creeping into her.

Everything rushed, way too fast. Police sealed the engineer's apartment, his possessions gone the next day; it stood empty, scrubbed clean, its bare walls echoing loss. Their embassy ordered them to serve authorities, refusing aid—communist regimes hand in hand, their intimidation bare. Police called Liana for interrogation, a cop toying with handcuffs, their clinking sharp in the dim room. They took Alina—half a day, horror gripping Liana—questioning all, pens scratching, their eyes stone. A gorilla in uniform—neck thick, forehead low—grilled Liana, hostile, scaring her cold. A Havana inspector, smiling, tried to soften his rudeness. Liana raged when the gorilla handed her a statement, twisting her words. "This is wrong!" she screamed. "I don't know why this is—no translator, no embassy! Don't try to pin this crime on my people—find the real killer!" she yelled, her rights violated, fearing arrest, Alina lost forever. The inspector stepped in, forcing a correct statement. Leaving, Liana cursed Cuba, the day they came. Then she saw their Cuban friends outside, their smiles breathing courage, their love for her family lifting her, real proof that life endures beyond regimes.

The embassy ghosted them, the endless ringing of their phones mocking their pleas. To send the engineer's body home, Cubans found no suit—his tall, strong frame unmatched, his possessions sealed, his apartment's locked door a silent taunt. The embassy refused—"No money," said the same men with dollars, credit cards that Liana never knew, their Mercedes engines purring past their grief. Liana couldn't shake the gut-punch: both communist governments schemed together, sweeping the murder under the rug. The investigation vanished, erased by some magic wand, its absence a heavy quiet in the air, a veil of silence over a heinous crime.

Defeated, they kept calling, begging for escape, each unanswered call a weight on Liana's chest. Then, their plane tickets landed, months of pleas answered, the paper crisp in Liana's trembling hands. On the plane to Havana, another man in a white guayabera with a heavy briefcase avoided eye contact, his cologne sharp in the stale cabin air. They didn't know if he was watching them, but it felt wrong.

In all this, the city rallied around them. The day before their flight to Havana, friends poured in. Their memories burned heavy, but love burned stronger. The doctor, their savior, held them close, his warmth a gift, his gentle hands lingering on Alina's head, his eyes soft with the bond they'd forged through epidemics and shared whispers. Marko's coworkers gripped hands, voices cracked with farewells, their calloused palms a testament to the roads they'd built together, the blueprints now gathering dust.

Alina tugged Liana outside, dust gritty under her sandals, and what Liana saw seared into her soul: thirty kids lined up in the dust, sobbing, barefoot in clean rags, waiting to say goodbye. Each kissed Liana, their lips warm, their small arms wrapping around her waist, their tears soaking her dress. The sweet girl, five or six now, grasped Liana, crying, "Mommy, don't leave!" Her arms were fierce and desperate, and Liana broke. Her tears spilled, love hurting deep, a scar that never heals. The children's hugs were a tidal wave of emotion, their dirty hands clutching her skirt, their voices a chorus of pleas—"Stay, Mami!" "Don't go!"—their bonds forged in dust and games, Alina's "sister" among them, her face crumpled with loss. Liana's state of mind fractured—guilt for leaving these little ones who'd become her family, their laughter her salve against Cuba's cruelties, their hugs a reminder of the light they'd brought to her exile. The doctor stood nearby, his exhaustion masked by a smile, his "They love you" a quiet acknowledgment of the bond she'd built, his own affection a flame she felt but left unspoken. Marko's hand on her shoulder was a steady anchor, his silence a shared ache for the home they'd found despite the blood.

Liana knelt, her knees in the dust, hugging each child, their small bodies trembling against hers, their scents of sweat and earth a memory she'd carry forever. "I'll miss you all," she whispered, her voice breaking, her heart torn between the pull of home and the love she'd grown in this dust-bound cage. The sweet girl's hug lingered the longest, her "*Te quiero, Mami*" a knife in Liana's chest, her tears hot on Liana's neck. The bond with these friends—the doctor, the architect, Rosa, the coworkers—was a fire that had sustained her, their kindness a light against the regime's shadow, their shared stories a tapestry of resistance she'd weave into her future. As the kids clung, Liana's resolve hardened—she'd fight to return, to bring them gifts of freedom, her mind already planning letters, packages, a bridge across oceans. The farewell stretched, the sun dipping low, casting long shadows that mirrored her sorrow, but in their eyes, she saw hope, a spark she'd nurture from afar.

At the airport, by the looming ladder, Marko's colleagues stood, farewells tangled with tears. Liana hugged the doctor—his smile so gentle, his daily sacrifice for children's health a ray of brightest light—and sobbed, "No one's ever touched our hearts like you." Desperate, Liana realized she wanted to stay. Guantánamo was their home, despite the blood. But he pushed her to go. Love won in the end, despite knives, threats, and lies—a spark pulling them to Matanzas years later, bound to Cuba forever.

HELLO MATANZAS

Liana leaned back as the IL-62's thunderous roar shook the cabin, air thick with electricity. Flight attendants forced tight smiles, their tension spiking Liana's. A stewardess passed candies, their wrappers crinkling faintly, but Liana waved her off, her stomach too knotted. She'd flown Cubana for years, each trip worse, the planes shakier, the fear sharper. Liana hated flying—dreaded heights, loathed losing control—but today, her usual panic vanished. Even the antique Soviet machine's frightening whine, rattling the fuselage, its metallic groan piercing her ears, didn't faze her.

They were returning to Cuba after being away for years. Guantánamo's scars lingered—murder, betrayal—but love pulled Liana and Marko back. The dust of Guantánamo had clung to Liana's skin like a second shadow, its grit a reminder of those few unforgivable years—roaches skittering in the dark, jets roaring low over their shack, the engineer's blood staining the morgue's cold tiles, his sunshine smile silenced forever. Cuba had not been the salvation they'd dreamed, its socialist promises crumbling like Havana's colonial facades, yet its people—the doctor's gentle hands mending Alina's cough, the children's gap-toothed grins chasing her through the dust, the little girl begging her not to leave—had woven a bond stronger than the regime's chains. Liana, Marko, and Alina had survived, their hearts scarred but fierce, carrying the weight of love and loss as they left Guantánamo behind. The Skoda Octavia, frog-green and rattling, had carried them through barbed wire and mine warnings, its torn seats soaked with the memory of a desperate mother's wail, a baby offered in despair, her sobs echoing in Liana's dreams. That road had ended, but the pull of Cuba, its warmth and pain, lingered like the humid air on Liana's skin, a siren's song that called them back despite the blood and betrayal.

When Marko was offered Matanzas, they hesitated. So much had gone wrong there—blood, fear, and loss. Liana worried, her heart heavy, unsure what lay ahead. Back home, cracks split the Eastern European socialist bloc, whispers of revolt humming like a distant storm, but liberty felt years away. Cuba was different. Castro's steel fist starved people, watched every word and step, his propaganda posters glaring from every wall, and crushed dissent with cruel precision—lauding traitors' punishment as a warning to all.

They packed again, their bags heavier with memory—Alina's doll, now worn from hugs, soap bars stacked like bricks against the unknown, a photograph of the guava tree Liana had hacked from the dust, its branches a fleeting triumph over the overall neglect.

José Martí Airport's new metal structure gleamed, its cold steel walls echoing footsteps, but customs hadn't changed. Long lines exhausted them. The endless flight in that shaking airplane left them raw. They took Liana's passport, which explicitly stated she could visit only Cuba. No Madrid this time—her aunt's visit years ago was deemed disobedience by the communist authorities. At Customs, they waved every piece of clothing in the air, fabric flapping like flags of shame, expecting secrets to fall. They rummaged through Liana's panties and bras, ripping open a delicate, feminine package. Liana's face burned crimson, sweat prickling her skin, her voice trembling as she protested their invasion. No reaction. The officer's stone face moved to Alina's books. A commotion erupted nearby—a young Cuban student's tiny American flag was torn from his shirt, the rip sharp in the humid air, and they dragged him away, with no welcome flowers in sight. Then Customs fixated on Alina's bubble gum, wrapped in foil from the flight. Bubble gum was rare back home; Liana had spent her few U.S. dollars at the duty-free shop for Alina's treat. They inspected the tiny ball as if it hid a bomb. Liana stared in disbelief —what could anyone conceal in there? Alina, tall and slim, her blond hair spilling over her arms, took revenge. She never forgot the peach ripped from her mouth in Guantánamo, leaving her in tears. Now, calm and smiling, she clutched an apple as they reached for it. "With your permission," she said in perfect Spanish, biting deep, its crisp juice bursting on her tongue, chewing with delight. The officer nearly cracked their passports with his seal, the stamp's thud echoing, and they were free to enter Cuba again. Marko waited, kisses flew, and they headed to Matanzas.

The ocean roared, overpowering the Malecón. Few cars passed, their engines coughing in the heat, and people in old but clean clothes smiled politely. Warmth filled Liana's heart. No matter the regime, Cubans gave them love and hope, even in their darkest moments. Matanzas hit Liana hard—she expected Guantánamo's fire, but its colors were softer, faded like sun-bleached cloth, less vibrant than Oriente's splendor. Small houses lined the road, each unique, with palm-leaf roofs, their brittle edges rustling in the breeze, like relics from a century past. As they climbed the final hill on Via Blanca, a thermoelectric plant's chimney loomed to the left. A suffocating white cloud swallowed them, its acrid stench burning Liana's throat. They coughed, wiping away tears, then Matanzas Bay opened below, its blue waters inviting, sparkling under a salty breeze caressing a nearly deserted harbor. They reached their new home, a cluster of Z-shaped, five-story buildings for foreign specialists, with aluminum blinds and—finally—window air conditioners, their hum a faint promise of relief. They clustered them again—easier to watch and control.

Liana flung open the balcony door, the ocean's salt hitting her face, then froze—a naked couple entangled next door, moaning, for all to see and hear. Terrified, Liana slammed the door shut, its hinges squeaking, closed the blinds, and grabbed Alina. "Let's check the ocean," she said, but guards stopped them at the exit for orientation, their boots scuffing the concrete. The complex was for Westerners and workers paid in U.S. dollars only. As the first Eastern European bloc family stuck with Cuban pesos, they were barred from the restaurant and the post office. The ritual dragged—rules on pesos, dollar-payers only for restaurant and post office, their Eastern European bloc status a mark of exclusion. Liana's blood boiled—the system embracing some like a mother, others like a cold mother-in-law. Nearby houses, poor with seas of antennas swaying in the humid wind, mirrored their abandonment, a chill settling in Liana's bones despite the heat. Alina tugged her hand, her doll dangling loosely. "Mommy, why can't we go?" Liana knelt, "Soon, sweetheart," her voice steady, her heart heavy with the divide. The guards' eyes lingered, a reminder of the eyes that never slept, but Liana's resolve hardened, a spark from her Eastern European past now burning in Cuba's hostile ground.

The next week, they drove to Havana to register Alina for school. Marko scored a gas coupon—rationing still ruled—and they took Via Blanca. No air conditioning, they opened the windows, letting the breeze swirl, warm and sticky on their skin. Then a white cloud from a factory called Rayonera choked them, the air stinging Liana's nose—thick with oil and decay. They couldn't breathe, couldn't see. The three of them coughed, tears streaming, trapped in the car. Liana tore off her shirt, pressing it to Alina's face, its rough cotton damp with sweat. Marko sped up, half-blind, praying that they wouldn't crash. Few cars dotted the road—rentals, buses, and police. Havana's decay hit hard—its crumbling streets a slap after Matanzas's quiet. Buildings, gray and peeling, their plaster flaking like dead skin, only hinted at their old glory. Balconies crumbled in the salty air, Spanish colonial gems dying from neglect. Police and military swarmed, their boots a warning to stay silent, batons tapping rhythmically. Huge signs screamed socialism's triumph, Castro's menacing finger plastered everywhere, faded red ink bleeding in the sun. Long waits for a sandwich—if any—stretched even longer for coffee, its bitter steam a fleeting tease. Coppelia's ice cream, a hunger's only balm, took ninety minutes to reach, its sugary chill a rare escape.

The Ministry of Education sat in a baroque relic, its "imperialist"-era leftover furniture stained and battered, dust motes dancing in slanted light. They registered Alina and, thrilled, headed to the Riviera, an American-built hotel still mostly intact, its polished floors gleaming under faded chandeliers. At the restaurant, tired and hungry, a guard heard they paid in pesos and pointed to the door, his voice sharp as a slammed gate. No plea worked—the dollar ruled. At Cubalse, Santiago de Cuba's twin, shelves overflowed for dollar-holders, bright packages mocking their empty hands. They tried for pizza. Alina's sad face, hungry and rejected, broke Liana's heart, her eyes glistening in the harsh fluorescent glow. The cashier, moved, got permission to sell one slice for pesos, its greasy warmth a small victory. Liana felt tired, upset, and disenfranchised. For the millionth time, she saw it—a divide split not by merit but by birth and luck.

School started with uniforms, red scarves, and mandatory communist oaths, their chants echoing like Liana's childhood's forced hymns. True to her Guantánamo roots, Alina brought home two classmates, their laughter spilling through their cramped apartment. The administration warned Liana: no Cuban kids allowed. Her blood boiled. "But prostitutes are welcome, correct?"

she snapped, recalling the girls parading nightly since their arrival, their cheap perfume lingering in the halls. "We'll make an exception," they said, but Liana sensed more fights ahead.

The complex housed mostly single Yugoslavs and their French bosses, some of whom had families. They worked on a new supertanker terminal—a socialist flop, barely used except for small tankers. Liana watched them toil, 24/7 shifts under the sun, sweat soaking their shirts, hammers clanging against steel, packed into the overpriced restaurant they couldn't enter. Their sweat meant nothing—the terminal sat nearly empty, a symbol of Castro's failed plans, its rusted cranes creaking in the wind. Only Spain's oil pipeline to the thermoelectric plant was done—no tanks or pipeline to Cienfuegos were yet built, leaving their labor a hollow boast. Their dollars fueled another scourge—prostitution. The French bosses kept to themselves, aloof from workers and Cubans, except for short-term visitors without spouses. Then more girls came to the complex, young and every shade, selling their youth for clothes, food, or dollars, their heels clicking on the concrete at dusk. Many doubled as police informants—spies in plain sight. The same tactics Liana had seen at home—informants, control—still haunted today's liberal playbooks. No difference from her country; the communist script never changed.

Sexually transmitted diseases spread unchecked, a silent plague fueled by the prostitution rampant in their complex. Liana saw it daily—young girls trading their youth for dollars, their eyes hollow, their futures stolen. Then Liana's own body betrayed her. Harsh detergent, the only kind they could get, burned her hands raw—bloody wounds splitting the skin between her fingers, deteriorating fast. The burn spread like wildfire, red welts cracking open, stinging with every move. Liana's hands became a map of pain. She soaked them in boiling water, the steam rising like a veil, but the wounds deepened, and pus oozed yellow. Scared, Liana headed to the hospital—lines snaking long, air thick with sweat and fear, disinfectant's sharp bite stinging her nose. Her Yugoslav neighbors were there too, shifting away from her, their eyes dodging hers, their faces flushed under the dim fluorescent buzz. It hit Liana hard —detergent wasn't their problem. Their shame screamed what they hid: infections from the same dark trade Liana had seen night after night. Liana waited, Alina at her side, her doll resting in her lap, her small fingers tracing Liana's bandages. "Does it hurt, Mommy?" she asked, her voice small. "A little," Liana lied, her heart aching at Alina's concern. A doctor appeared at the end of the line, his face gray with exhaustion, his hands waving her forward. "Let me see," he said, his voice low, his fingers gentle as he examined the wounds. "Infection," he murmured, his eyes meeting hers with worry, his care a steady light. He prescribed antibiotics and salve, his "Be careful, keep your hands wrapped, the infection can spread," his advice a hidden threat. Back home, the salve soothed, but her Yugoslav neighbors' flushed faces haunted her—their shame a mirror to the complex's dark trade, a plague spreading silently.

Back home, Christmas neared. Liana and Alina brought ornaments this time, and their tree lit up the apartment, its pine scent a faint echo of home. Gifts waited for Alina, but her school friends had none, their bare homes silent under Castro's shadow. Cubans had nothing but Castro's endless, unhinged speeches, his voice droning through crackling TVs. They couldn't escape his rants, their screens blaring. Liana and Marko unplugged theirs, craving silence—Cubans couldn't afford even that.

MORE HYSTERIA

School brought hate. Cuban kids were taught day after day, voices shrill in crowded classrooms. The hate was white-hot, aimed at the U.S. and the "*gusanera*" in Miami—worms, a slur spat like venom. Many couldn't read or write after years in school, the chalk dust clouding desks, and education drowned in political brainwashing. Hours were spent singing praises to Castro and the revolution, hymns echoing off cracked walls, more hours in school plazas under the blistering sun, innocents poisoned by endless propaganda, words droning like a swarm of flies.

Alina's school days began with the red scarf, its fabric rough against her neck, the chants a daily ritual that left her voice hoarse. Liana walked her to the gate, concrete hot under their sandals, air thick with chalk and sweat. The teacher, her hair pulled tight, eyes sharp, greeted them with a nod—her "Good morning" a command. Alina's hand slipped from Liana's, doll tucked in her bag, steps hesitant as she joined the line. The courtyard filled with children, uniforms faded, shoes worn, voices rising in the morning hymn—a sound that grated Liana's ears. Alina's friend, a thin girl with braids, waved, her smile a light in the gray, but the teacher's glare silenced her. Liana watched from the fence, her heart heavy, the children's faces a mix of boredom and fear, eyes already learning to look away. Alina turned once, "Bye, Mommy," a whisper, her blonde hair catching the sun, a spark in the morning. Liana waved, her smile forced, her mind racing with the teacher's words, the hate poured into young hearts. The bell rang, a harsh clang, and the children filed in, their footsteps a march, Liana's worry a weight she carried home.

Day after day, the school courtyard baked under the midday sun, concrete cracked like old skin, children lined up in rows, with red scarves fluttering in the hot breeze. The teacher stood on a platform, her voice a whip: "Repeat after me: The worms in Miami are traitors!" The children chanted, their voices a dull roar, some stumbling over the words, eyes vacant. Liana watched from the gate, her heart twisting as Alina stood among them, her blonde hair a stark contrast, her small mouth moving with the crowd. The teacher paced, her sandals slapping the ground, her eyes scanning for any child who hesitated, her finger pointing like a gun. "Louder!" she barked, and the chant rose, a wave of hate crashing against the faded walls. Liana's stomach churned—this was no education, just poison poured into young minds, their innocence drowned in the heat. Alina's friend, the thin girl with braids, whispered to her, "My cousin sends me candy from Miami," her voice a secret, her eyes darting. The teacher caught it, her "Silence!" a slap, the girl's face paling as she shrank back. Liana's hands clenched, the memory of her own childhood chants a bitter echo, but here, the venom was sharper, the children's eyes already hardening.

Teaching kids to hate relatives in Miami or the U.S. wasn't easy —money and presents flowed from America to the impoverished island, their priceless packages crinkling with hope. Those with family there were blessed, getting dollars, clothes, or shoes. It struck Liana when Alina shared how the teacher demanded her class stand

and shout hate for those "worms" in Miami, her voice barking over the room's stale air. One girl rose and said, "Professor, I can't hate my aunt—she sends me shoes, I love her." It echoed Liana's love for her aunt in Madrid, before she ever met her—she had sent the shimmering fabric for Liana's prom dress, the silk cool against her fingers. Liana still recalled the sheer joy of wearing it, music humming in the warm night. No, humans are meant to love, not hate, especially their kin. Explaining this to Alina was tough; her brow furrowed in the dim lamplight, but she understood, like most kids. They knew hate was wrong, yet the crime of poisoning young souls persisted in Cuba's schools.

One day, watching the kids leave school, Liana saw Alina covered in blood, red streaks matting her blonde hair. Liana's heart stopped. She ran down the stairs, steps creaking under her weight, grabbed Alina, screaming where she was hurt—who did this? No wounds—it was the regime's hysteria. Schools staged U.S. Army invasions, fake explosions rumbling the ground, planes dropping bombs, destroying homes, schools, and roads. Children were thrown into panic, doused with aseptil rojo over heads and bodies. They had to crawl under elevated schools, with dirt scraping knees, among scorpions, snakes, and iguanas, hiding from Yankees, the dust choking their throats. Jets booming overhead or sirens breaking the ocean's hum froze them, wails slicing the humid air, never knowing what came next. Alina's clothes were stained, her hair messy, her legs scratched, but she was safe. Still, the ordeal scarred her young mind. It took time to soothe her, her trembling hands clutching Liana's, convincing her that she, her schoolmates, and they weren't in danger.

Another time the invasion drill came without warning, the school's siren a wail that cut through the morning heat, children scrambling from their desks, their chairs scraping the floor. Alina's teacher barked orders, her voice a whip, "Under the building! Now!" The children ran, their sandals slapping the concrete, their cries a chorus of fear. Alina's hand found her friend's, their fingers interlaced, their faces pale as they crawled into the dust, the ground hot under their knees, scorpions skittering in the shadows. The aseptil rojo poured from buckets, its red liquid sticky on their skin, matting Alina's hair, staining her uniform. "The Yankees are coming!" the teacher shouted, her voice frantic, the fake explosions rumbling, dust choking their throats. Alina's doll fell from her bag, its fabric soaked in red, its button eyes staring up at the chaos. Liana waited outside, her heart pounding, the siren's wail a knife in her chest, the children's cries echoing from under the building. When they emerged, Alina's face was streaked with red, her legs scratched, her eyes wide with terror. Liana ran to her, her arms a haven, her "You're safe" a whisper against the horror. The teacher's "Good job" was a slap, the children's faces hollow, their innocence drowned in the red.

While Alina enjoyed her schoolmates, Liana and Marko made friends, happy to share meals, plates clinking in their cramped kitchen, their company a balm. Inviting them was hard—they had to leave their IDs at reception, with passes that Liana and Marko signed, the ink smudging under sweaty fingers. Risks grew when the socialist bloc crumbled, branding them enemies of the revolution. The complex got its new ex-State Security administrator, boots thudding with menace, who cranked surveillance to a fever pitch. No kids could visit without permission, their laughter silenced by the gate. Liana's heart ached—Alina's friends, their gap-toothed grins, their games in the dust, were a light in the gray, but the administrator's eyes, cold and unblinking, watched every move.

The friends came despite the rules, their footsteps soft on the concrete, their voices low as they slipped past the gate. Liana's kitchen filled with their warmth, the clink of plates a rhythm of normalcy, the scent of rice and beans a comfort in the heat. Alina's laughter rang, her friends' hands sticky with mango, their games a spark in the cramped space. Liana watched from the doorway, her heart lifting, the administrator's shadow a weight she pushed away. The ex-State Security man paced the hall, his boots a thud, his eyes scanning, his presence a chill. "No visitors," he barked one day, his voice a slap, but Liana's "They're family" was a defiance, her Spanish steady. The friends came anyway, their hugs a rebellion, their stories a light against the surveillance. Marko shared stories, his voice low, the terminal's flop a joke they laughed at, their bond a fire no administrator could snuff. Alina's friend, the girl with braids, brought her smile, her "For you, Mami," a gift, her eyes bright. Liana's heart swelled, the love a balm, but the administrator's knock, his "Papers" a demand, cut the joy short, his eyes lingering on the children's faces, a reminder of the eyes that never slept.

The French and Yugoslavs left, replaced by Indians and Eastern European bloc families. Kids swarmed, their endless laughter a bright spark, speaking different tongues yet bonding easily, making Liana wonder why adults couldn't achieve the same. The administrator lost his cool, his shouts echoing in the courtyard as he banned kids from outside apartments. Imprisoning children? In Soviet style, he called a residents' meeting, chairs scraping concrete, to enforce his rules. He didn't know Eastern European women wouldn't bow to insanity. As Liana raised her voice with other mothers, anger burning her throat, a precocious boy, fearless with insects, threw a rat at him, a squeak piercing the air. Laughter erupted, echoing off Z-shaped buildings, the man fuming, unused to defiance. Triumphantly, kids kept running, making noise, the boy charming all, his grin wide as he showed Liana lizards and cockroaches dangling proudly.

A new friend appeared—a mild-mannered policeman, his badge glinting faintly. Liana doubted it was by chance, but they bonded, his soft laugh warming their table, obeying rules, and signing passes. Over months, he opened up, his voice low in the humid dusk, an honest friend, not just snooping. One day, he offered to take them to Boca de Camarioca, a paradise for Communist Party elites, with waves lapping white sand, accessible only to military or police. "Like home," Liana thought, memories of restricted resorts stinging, but different. His bringing them was an unforgivable sin —guards' eyes narrowing—they turned back, never seeing him at their home again. Later, they learned he paid dearly for bringing foreigners to land forbidden to ordinary people, his silhouette fading in the dusty street. From afar, he'd avoid them, crossing roads, his steps quick to guard his fragile future. At least he didn't disappear like Marko's coworker, forcibly taken by the regime and vanished forever.

Varadero was similar—a coastal gem, with sand glowing white, the ocean a celestial blue, but off-limits to Cubans. They couldn't enjoy their own land, barriers glinting with exclusion. Liana, Marko, and Alina savored Sundays there, the waves cool against their skin, walking miles into transparent water, with shells and fish vivid. They used peso-accepting restaurants, spices lingering on tongues, grateful yet unable to condone the regime's barriers. They'd sneak Cuban friends in, the guards' grumbles ignored, their small rebellion against discriminatory rules.

Driving to the beach one day, Alina craved a fresco. They stopped at a Varadero shop, the wooden counter weathered, watching her, barefoot, sun-darkened, blonde hair swaying, in her tiny bathing suit. She stormed back, eyes blazing with disgust: "They said Cubans aren't allowed!" They laughed—her Spanish so flawless that none guessed she wasn't local—her small fists clenched, a child's fury at rejection. Liana got the fresco, its icy chill, a brief comfort, pondering why Cubans were barred from their land, the ocean's roar mocking exclusion.

They couldn't speak of hunger, shortages, coupons, restrictions, or police fear, with batons glinting under Havana's sun. In Havana, Liana saw police chase two women, beating them with batons, cracks echoing in the crowded street, and throwing them into a car.

Speechless, scared—heart pounding—Liana thought, what if that was them? Alina? The horror tormented her. Liana was rebellious, Alina no different, her defiance sharp as her mother's. Marko tempered their fire, his calm voice a steady anchor, until months later they realized danger had brushed them, escaping by miracle, fear lingering like damp heat.

Restrictions choked them. The postal service faltered; phoning Liana's parents was near impossible. One day, a knock—Liana's mother calling the administration, her voice a faint lifeline. Liana ran downstairs, floorboards creaking, grabbed the phone, its worn plastic heavy in her hand, eager for her voice, a balm to her ears. "Hey Mommy, I love you, I miss you, are you all fine?" Liana said, words straining through static, fighting thousands of miles and bad reception. Her mother said Liana's father had died. Liana couldn't believe it, didn't want to, tears burning her eyes. Between sobs and questions, the line cut, with silence heavy as grief. Liana stood, phone in hand, her world sinking, numb, hurting, unable to tell Alina, her love for her grandpa fierce in her faithful heart. Liana had promised her father a warm winter coat—"I'm so sorry, Daddy, I failed," she thought, her guilt raw.

Later, Liana learned her mother tried for a week to reach them, Cuba blocking calls, each failed attempt a stab. Heartbroken, Liana mourned her hero, tortured by communists, his scars rough under her childhood touch, and Alina's sweet grandpa, weaving tales of ninety-nine bears, his voice soft in the evening glow, to coax her stubborn appetite. That severed connection, dusk's chill settling in Liana's bones, mirrored the regime's silencing of dissent, a cruelty she'd soon see writ large.

The regime's grip tightened beyond their walls, crushing dissent with an iron hand. Hundreds of political prisoners—writers, dreamers, and rebels—languished in hidden cells, chains clanking in the damp dark, their voices silenced for daring to speak truth. Liana had heard whispers of their fate, families' sobs echoing in dusty alleys, wives and children left to beg for news that never came. It chilled her—her fear sharp as a blade—knowing any misstep could land them there, Alina's laughter snuffed out. Back home, Liana had seen jails swallow the brave, her father's scars a silent testament, and Cuba's prisons were no different, a shadow haunting every rebellious thought.

The world began to notice Cuba's cruelty, the United Nations calling out its human rights abuses—prisoners' silenced cries echoing beyond the island. Castro answered with a four-hour tirade, shouts crackling through radios, more unhinged than ever, flailing wildly, spewing venom at the United States, United Nations, and Eastern European bloc, blaming them for Cuban blood in a phantom U.S. invasion. His words turned Liana, Marko, and Alina into "enemies of the revolution," a noose tightening around their necks, dread heavy in the humid air, its weight suffocating their fragile hope. Alina's laughter, their small rebellions, now felt like targets, fear pulsing through their shack, a shadow they couldn't outrun.

ENEMY OF THE REVOLUTION

It was time for a quick vacation back home—a turbulent, exciting time, the cracks in the socialist bloc growing, winds of change whistling through the streets. People's euphoria reached a crescendo, filling hearts with hope for a better future, banners flapping in the crisp air.

The flight home was a blur of turbulence and tears, the plane's engines coughing like the old Skoda, the cabin air stale with recycled breath. Liana clutched Alina's hand, her small fingers warm, her doll resting in her lap, her eyes wide with the promise of home. The terminal was a blur of faces, the air sharp with winter's bite, the banners of change flapping in the wind. Then she saw her mother—standing at the gate, her black dress a shadow against the gray, her eyes hollow with grief, her arms open. Liana ran, Alina's hand slipping from hers, her "Grandma!" a cry that cut through the noise. The hug was fierce, Liana's tears soaking her mother's shoulder, Alina's small body pressed between them, her "I missed you" a whisper that mended the dark. The airport's concrete was cold under their feet, the air sharp with coal and hope, the banners a light in the gray. Liana's mother held them close, her "My girls" a balm, her grief a weight they shared, the loss of Liana's father a silence that hung between them.

Liana's mother's apartment was a faded sanctuary, its walls cracked from years of neglect, the air heavy with the scent of boiled cabbage and grief. The furniture, worn from use, sagged under their weight; the single bulb cast long shadows across the table where family photos spoke of endless love. Alina ran through the rooms, her doll tucked under her arm, her "It's big!" a joy that pierced the sorrow. Liana's mother sat, her black dress absorbing the light, her hands trembling as she poured tea from a cracked pot, the steam rising like a veil. "He waited for you," she whispered, her voice breaking, her eyes red from nights of crying. Liana's throat closed, the memory of her father's scarred hands, his gentle stories of ninety-nine bears, an ache that swelled in her chest. Alina climbed into her lap, her "Grandpa?" a question that hung in the air, her small fingers tracing the photo. Liana's mother nodded, tears spilling, her "He loved you both" a whisper that broke them. The evening stretched, the silence broken by Alina's questions, her innocence a light in the dark, Liana's mother sharing stories of his last days, his "Tell Liana to keep fighting" a final command. Liana held Alina close, her heart raw, the grief a wave that crashed over them, the hope of change a distant light.

The next day, Alina and Liana hit the streets, joining every rally, their fists in the air, screaming "No communism again!" Voices hoarse, they roared with the crowd, claiming their place under the sun, a part of history's making. Years in school taught to hate, Alina hiding under the school from imaginary Yankee invasions, scorpions skittering in the dark, Liana's father's torture, their friend's death by an unknown murderer—memories boiled inside, rage burning Liana's throat, losing her voice, holding signs high, telling the world, "See us, two generations of women fighting for freedom!"

The rallies were a storm of voices, the streets packed with

people, the air thick with the scent of sweat and hope. Liana and Alina marched, their signs held high, the paint still wet, the words a scream against the gray. The crowd surged, their chants a wave, the banners flapping like wings, the police watching from the edges, their faces stone. Alina's hand was warm in Liana's, her “Freedom!” a shout that rose above the noise, her blonde hair a flag in the wind. The speakers stood on platforms, their voices raw, their words a fire that lit the crowd, the stories of prisons and torture a weight that fueled the rage. Liana's throat burned, her voice gone, but her heart roared, the memory of her father's scars a fuel, the engineer's blood a stain she couldn't wash away. Alina's friend from school—the girl whose ponytail the policemen cut years ago—marched beside them, her “No more!” a defiance that made Liana's eyes tear. The crowd moved, their footsteps a drum, the signs a forest of hope, the future a light at the end of the tunnel. Liana's mother watched from the window, her black dress a shadow, her smile a light in the dark, her “Go, my girls” a whisper that carried them forward.

Through it all, Liana and Marko clung to their marriage like a raft in the storm. They had vowed to shield Alina from the weight of their scars, to give her a childhood uncracked by the world's cruelty. Every night, they tucked her in, her worn doll resting beside her, her “Good night, Mommy and Daddy” a light in the dark. Liana read her stories, her voice soft, the words a shield against the chants and the hunger. Marko sang her the old songs, his voice hoarse from the day's shouts, his hand on her forehead a promise. They cooked together, the kitchen cramped, the scent of rice and beans a comfort, their laughter a defiance. Alina's joy was their oxygen, her gap-toothed grin a spark that kept them going. They promised each other—whatever came, they would keep her childhood whole, her heart unburdened by the world's hate.

It wasn't rosy. Communists in Liana's country derailed democracy, changing skins like chameleons. Back in Havana, the embassy panicked, phones ringing endlessly, bureaucrats scrambling to secure privileges, their shiny Mercedes, dollars, and expensive residences. When Liana and Marko asked about the investigation into their friend's murder, their frozen stares met them, fingers jabbing the air, warning silence, stunned by their perceived arrogance to even ask. Nobody cared then; nobody cared now. Dollar stores stood empty, Noriega's absence screaming from bare counters, now lined with guayaberas and the same greenish butterfly floaties. Local shops displayed empty boxes, shelves stark under flickering bulbs, a scary void.

Soon, Castro held another rally with a hours-long speech—one of those never-ending rants, cursing imperialism, blaming others for his failures, his voice booming through crackling speakers, beaming pride for his crisis solution: animal traction. No petroleum, no gas, no problem!—bicycles clattering, horse buggies creaking—filled the streets. Horses defecated everywhere, the stench thick in the humid air, millions of fleas trailing, resting on bread in carriages, crusts gritty with filth. People sold heirloom jewelry for food, rings glinting in desperate hands. Mothers sold daughters to foreigners for scraps, their sobs muffled in the night. Empty stores, refrigerators, and bellies. Silence—forced silence—for millions of hungry Cubans.

Castro's speech was a marathon of venom, his voice crackling through the radio, his words a storm that drowned the hope. Liana sat in the kitchen, the radio's static a hiss, his "Animal traction!" a boast that made her stomach turn. The streets filled with bicycles, their bells a frantic chime, the horse buggies creaking under their loads, the stench of manure a cloud that followed them. The bread in the carriages, its crusts gritty with fleas, was a meal for the desperate, the mothers' sobs a sound that haunted the night. Liana's hands shook as she turned off the radio, the silence a relief, the hunger a weight pressing on her chest. Alina's school friends, their bellies empty, their eyes hollow, were a mirror to the crisis, their "I'm hungry" a whisper that broke Liana's heart. Liana's resolve hardened, her love for Cuba a fire that burned despite the hunger, the silence a chain she would break.

The rally stretched into the night, the plaza packed with bodies, the air thick with sweat and dust, the loudspeakers crackling with Castro's voice, his words a hammer that pounded the crowd. Liana stood at the edge of the couch, Alina asleep on her shoulder, her small body warm, her breathing steady against the roar blaring from the TV screen. The people clapped, their hands raw, their faces blank, their eyes fixed on the stage, the leader's shadow long in the floodlights. The bicycles clattered past, their riders' faces gaunt, their legs pumping in rhythm, the horse buggies creaking behind, their drivers' whips cracking the air. The horses neighed, their eyes wild, their hooves slipping on the cobblestones, the manure piling high, the stench a fog that clung to clothes and skin. The bread sellers moved through the crowd, their trays empty, their voices hoarse, their "Pan! Pan!" a plea that went unanswered. The jewelry sellers stood in the shadows, their rings glinting in the dim light, their faces lined with desperation, their "Gold for food" a whisper that cut through the noise.

Liana turned the TV off, Alina's weight a comfort, the streets outside dark, the silence a weight. The apartment was quiet, the air thick with the scent of rice and beans. Marko sat at the table, his face pale, his hands clenched, his "We can't stay" a whisper that hung in the air. Liana nodded, her heart heavy, the hunger a shadow that followed them. The neighbors knocked, their faces hollow, their "Do you have anything?" a plea that broke her heart. She gave them the last of the rice, the beans, the bread, their "Gracias," a light in the dark. The night stretched long, the silence a chain, the hunger a weight, the hope a spark that flickered in the dark.

Their Cuban friends felt sadness at the difference in how the regime treated them, yet, as in Guantánamo, they risked extending their love, offering solace with warm smiles, consoling Liana and

Marko when they were branded enemies. Liana always believed a country is more than borders or government—it's its people. Those hungry, oppressed men and women, hearts big despite empty pockets, without a future, made Cuba alive and lovely. Despite problems hitting from every side, their spirit unbroken, they smiled, laughed, found humor in daily struggles, and shared friendship with open hands, a gift to those in need.

Often, walking the streets, dust gritty under Liana's shoes, she watched them; as soon as they passed a cafeteria, speakers blasting salsa's vibrant beat, they danced, as if alone in the world, pure happiness in motion. It amazed Liana, their joy a spark she couldn't catch. She wondered why she couldn't drop her fears, forget everything, and join them, if only for a moment. But Liana was born with worry etched on her face, sealed in her soul, and as much as she tried to be Cuban for a day, a weight pulled her down, holding her back, her heart tethered to dread.

One day, communist leaders visited their complex to inaugurate the little children's play area, built by workers with extra weekend labor, their hammers echoing through humid dawns. They twisted the event into a celebration of the revolution's triumph, red flags flapping garishly, calling residents for a party, the crowd's murmurs heavy with unease. "Celebrate what?" Liana wondered, her stomach churning with disgust. A corner cafeteria sold coffee, sugary ice, and "hamburgers"—a grotesque exaggeration, the patties made of cow blood, dark and slick, reeking of iron, drained just shy of death. Barbarically made, many refused them, gagging at the metallic tang, but empty bellies didn't care. As the leaders entered the community's compound, Liana saw two big guys fighting over the last sandwich—their fists thudding, their shouts echoing in the dusty street. In just five minutes, police cars screeched, sirens piercing the air.

The leaders stood on the platform, their voices droning, their words a weight that pressed on the crowd. The children played on the new swings, their laughter a light in the gray, but the leaders' eyes were cold, their smiles forced. Liana watched, her heart heavy, the red flags a shadow, the party a mockery. The coffee was bitter, the ice melted, and the "hamburgers" a joke that made her stomach turn. The fight in the cafeteria was over in minutes, the men handcuffed, dragged away, their faces pale, their "I was hungry" a whisper that cut through the noise. The police cars screeched away, the sirens fading—order restored, the silence a weight.

As the leaders lauded the party's "groundbreaking victories," voices droning like flies in the courtyard of their buildings, they started jumping, claiming their hopping shook the U.S. with fear, their feet thumping the cracked pavement. Stunned, Liana ran upstairs, stairs groaning under her haste, to scribble this insanity in her Cuban manuscript, her pen scratching fiercely, too absurd, too pathetic to forget.

In schools, "Down with Fidel" signs appeared, scrawled defiantly in chalk. Kids voiced dissent against taught hate, their whispers bold in dusty plazas. Dissidents spoke out, their voices rising in the humid dusk. The response was swift—police swarmed, their batons glinting in the sun. Ortega lost in Nicaragua, Angola slipped away, and surviving Cuban soldiers returned, their boots heavy with defeat. Fear and terror thickened the air, a weight pressing their chests. Castro's military doctrine ruled, turning all into regime marionettes, the strings pulled tight.

The friends came despite the fear, their footsteps soft, their voices low, their love a light in the dark. Liana's kitchen was their haven, the clink of plates a rhythm, the scent of rice and beans a comfort. Alina's laughter rang, her friends' games a spark, their joy a defiance. Liana watched, her heart lifting, the administrator's shadow a weight she pushed away. The love was a fire, the friendship a light, the people a country.

Hysteria spilled over them. One day, Marko screamed, lifting a fresco case, his face contorted in pain, dropping it, and bending from agony. A hernia—needing urgent care. Liana and Marko ran to the city hospital, the doors creaking with neglect—no luck. Mass sepsis cases rendered the hospital temporarily closed.

The lines at Havana's hospitals grew longer, patients waiting days for care, corridors reeking of sweat and despair, and nurses' voices sharp with exhaustion. Doctors operated with flashlights, batteries fading in the dim light, delivering babies with water-washed instruments. Marko, with an acute hernia untreated, was turned away from everywhere, hope fading in the humid air. Thankfully, a nearby military hospital had served foreigners before —French and Yugoslavs. The military hospital was a fortress of concrete, its walls stained with salt, the air thick with the smell of disinfectant and fear. Liana and Marko waited, their hands clasped, the uniforms crowding them, their voices a bark. The triage was quick, the doctor's "Hernia" a diagnosis that cut through the noise, and the bed a relief in the chaos. Marko's face was pale, his pajamas thin, his fever a fire that burned his skin. Liana sat beside him, her hand in his, the monitors beeping a rhythm of hope. Then a general stormed in, his medals clinking, his "You leave—we don't treat enemies of the revolution" a slap that iced Liana's veins. Marko's face paled, his "I could die" a whisper that broke her heart. Liana screamed, her voice raw, the general's "Out!" a command that echoed in the hall. Silly her—they were enemies. Bending, Marko rose, took off his pajamas, his steps faltering, and they left, the hospital doors slamming behind them.

Days passed, his condition worsening, the hernia bulging grotesquely, the fever draining his strength, and sweat soaking his brow. After two weeks—centuries long—the city hospital reopened. At 6 a.m., they went, dawn's gray light chilling. The sight seared Liana's soul—the city hospital was a tomb of neglect, its corridors reeking of sweat and despair, a third-world nightmare, neglect everywhere. Cigarette butts piled up on floors, ash acrid in the air, the trash strewn. A man pushing an oxygen bottle crashed into intensive care doors, the metal clanging, revealing patients with open wounds, a woman brushing the floor, dust swirling in the dim light, the sheets as filthy as the tiles. Terrified for Marko, her heart pounding, Liana started crying. The nurse's "We have no pajamas" cut through her heart, and the surgery felt like a flickering hope. Liana waited, her hands clenched, trembling.

By 10 a.m., they found pajamas, threadbare and stained, and took him to surgery. An hour later, a nurse called Liana, her voice clipped. "I've no clean clothes or shoes," Liana said. "No need," she replied, escorting Liana to the "sterile" area, her dusty shoes trailing grit. Marko lay, an hour post-anesthesia—doctors had no sterile instruments. After three hours, the clock ticking like a bomb, a second anesthesia round, the surgery done, they ordered them home. Liana protested, her voice raw with panic, begging for one night's stay—nothing worked. Less than two hours post-open surgery, Marko walked to the car, pain etching his face, supported by Liana. She drove like a turtle, wheels jolting on endless holes, desperate to avoid bumps. At their building, no elevator—five flights of stairs, each step a looming threat. Liana ran crying to the administration, tears hot on her cheeks, and those wonderful people jumped to help. Held by two Cubans, their grips firm, Marko reached their apartment, bedded. The night stretched long, fever burning his skin, the days passing until the infection eased. The scar—huge, bulging, and visible through his pants—was a "triumph" of socialist medicine, a jagged mark of survival. The true triumph, to Liana, was that he lived—as an enemy of the revolution.

THE AMMONIAC ACCIDENT

Despite all the calamities in Cuban lives, people there had a distinct sense of humor. The famous Faro de Castillo del Morro lighthouse stood high, a steadfast guard over Havana's harbor, a symbol of the nation and a source of pride for a once-glorious history, its white walls cracked from salt and time, its beam a faint pulse in the humid night. One day, someone scrawled on its walls, "*El último que apague la luz*" (The last one to turn off the light), graffiti bold under the sun. The entire country buzzed, laughter erupting in crowded streets, a release when political and military hysteria grew insufferable.

The graffiti appeared overnight, the paint still wet, the words a scream against the gray. People saw it from the Malecón, the letters bold against the stone, the laughter of the fishermen, a wave that crashed against the rocks. The word spread, the streets alive with whispers, the joke a spark in the dark. The police came, their boots scuffing the concrete, their "Who did this?" a bark that cut through the noise. The graffiti was quickly cleaned, the crowd dispersed, their faces filled with laughter, yet their eyes bright with the secret. Liana's heart lifted, the humor a light in the gray, the people's spirit a fire that burned despite the weight. Alina's friend, the girl with braids, whispered the joke at school, her "The last one to turn off the light," a giggle that made Liana's eyes tear. The lighthouse stood, with the joke a memory that lingered for years to come.

A friend of Marko's decided to turn off his own light. He took a boat, oars slicing the dark water, aiming to conquer the 90 miles to freedom under night's cover. The friend was a good fisherman, his boat worn from years of use, its wood faded from salt and sun. He left at midnight, the moon a sliver in the sky, the water black and still. Liana and Marko watched from the shore, their hearts heavy, the oars a rhythm in the dark. The coast guard came, their boats fast, their lights a stab in the night, their "Stop!" a command that echoed across the water. The friend fought, his oars a weapon, his "Freedom!" a shout that cut through the noise. He didn't succeed—he was apprehended, his trail fading in the regime's *cárceles*, a shadow swallowed by silence. They never heard of him again.

Police beatings, home invasions, and arrests became daily news, batons thudding in narrow alleys. Marko gifted Liana a radio, a rare luxury, its static hum a lifeline. The radio was a worn box, its plastic cracked, its antenna bent, but still working—a real, well-made American radio saved from years ago, its static a hiss that filled the kitchen. Liana tuned it at night, the volume low, the voices from Miami a lifeline in the dark. The broadcasters' words were a fire, their "Freedom is near" a promise that lit up the gray. Liana's hands shook as she wrote the news in her manuscript, her pen scratching fiercely, the facts a weapon against the lies. The radio was a light, the news a fire, the hope a dream that bound them.

It was then that Liana's affair with world news began, listening to Miami stations day and night, voices from afar sparking hope, assuring freedom was near if they fought. Her life changed—she felt stronger, more secure, as if shielded by truth. Liana never lost her gratitude to those Miami broadcasters who battled for Cuba's liberation, their words a beacon. They revealed truths omitted from them—escapes to better lives, the Eastern European bloc's collapse—raw facts, not Cuba's sterile lies. Years later, Liana would wake up to the news, scrolling for the latest of America's pulse, the screen glowing with the world's beat. In America, colleagues sought Liana's updates, knowing she was "on top" of the news, a fire born from her father's Voice of America nights back home. Listening to Cubanísima and Radio Martí, Liana gathered hope, sharing it with Cuban friends at night, whispers fueling dreams of an end to horror.

News broke of a Havana medic, HIV-positive, isolated from the world, and locked in solitude. Cuba began building clinics for others with the virus, de facto prisons, despite propaganda claiming state-of-the-art treatment facilities. Returning Angola war veterans, many infected, filled these buildings, their walls trapping despair. Television showcased "sanatoriums," young Cubans weeping, barred from leaving. It was depressing, the regime denying AIDS' existence in the open. A Cuban doctor friend, eyes weary, regretted not being HIV-positive. "You're joking," Liana said, stunned. He had a wife and two daughters. "If I had AIDS, I'd have food daily," he said, his voice breaking. Liana's heart shattered—people dragging through hunger, unsure of tomorrow's meal, preferred a prison cell with food slid through a window, a grim trade for survival.

One night in bed, sirens from passing cars screamed, a chaotic wail shaking the walls—Via Blanca roared with unusual commotion. Morning brought grim news: a train hauling ammonia tanks had derailed, killing several, with chaos erupting. The city plunged into hysterical chaos, a 25-ton cistern leaking, poisoning a vast urban area with toxic fumes. The first five victims died in the hospital, moans echoing in crowded wards, dozens treated for respiratory damage, lungs burning, and throats raw from coughing. Ammonia's pungent stench seared eyes and noses, tears streaming for 48 hours, as people wheezed, some clutching burned skin, red and blistered from chemical exposure. Children, more vulnerable, gasped harder, their small lungs overwhelmed, while asthmatics choked, their faces twisted in panic. Liana feared an explosion, her heart pounding, the air thick with dread as the gas spread, choking Matanzas' streets. It took 48 hours to bring in a crane, its groan faint against the panic, to remove the cistern. The railroads, crumbling, abandoned to fate, lacked maintenance, and Cubanitro and Rayonera, producing ammonia, poisoned half of Matanzas, their safety protocols a myth. Thousands evacuated, many with chemical burns scarring their flesh, some facing long-term lung damage, a silent scar of the regime's neglect. Nearby waters turned deadly, fish floating lifeless in poisoned streams, ecosystems choked by ammonia's toxic grip, a hidden toll on Cuba's fragile nature. Accidents happen worldwide, but developed nations have protections—regulations, controls. Cuba's decay, a legacy of communist ineptitude, left them defenseless, the world's news reporting Matanzas' plight in stark headlines.

Worried that their parents knew of the accident, Liana and Marko ran to Havana, dust swirling in their wake, seeking a phone; Cuba blocked their calls. Liana begged their complex's administrator, her voice trembling, for phone access—"No, dollars only," he snapped, his glare cold. At Hotel Havana Libre, they tried calling, but the lines were dead. "Something with the satellites," the clerk said, always some excuse. They ran to the post office, its floors slick with wear, sending a telegraph: "We are alive, thank God," words to soothe Liana's mother and Marko's parents, a fragile thread of solace.

The ammonia accident halted the Pedraplen de Matanzas, meant to ease city traffic—or so they claimed. In truth, it was a hastily sketched line by a local engineer, his pen scratching harbor shores, connecting Matanzas' entrance and exit. Presented to Commander-in-Chief Castro during a visit, blessed by his signature, it launched the Pedraplen, with no hydrogeological survey, no blueprints, just fervor. Enthusiasm soared, crowds chanting under the sun. Soon, the Pedraplen became a sad pile of rubble—rocks and pipes baking under the relentless sun, no progress despite truckloads dumped at the site. Three palms, planted for Castro, withered in the heat, marked the "progress" of a paper project. People dubbed it Tuboplen, the pipes and stones a monument to communist ineptitude, the enthusiasm fading, a stark symbol of failure.

Many offices and plants began closing, some permanently—workers sent to harvest produce, hands calloused under the relentless sun. Every Tuesday turned into a grueling camp day, fields thick with dust, as Cuba grappled with not enough power or petroleum. The entire island shifted to a grim survival mode—so-called "safe" and energy-saving—and in their complex, maintenance faithfully followed suit, ordered to grow garlic, its sharp scent clinging to sweaty clothes. Whispers spread that petrol reached the terminals, tankers clanging at dawn, only to disappear afterward, siphoned off by unseen hands. Foreign specialists in their complex confirmed this, their hushed voices tense, but it changed nothing—cars sat unused, rusting in silence, gas station tanks bone-dry, a stark emblem of the regime's deceit.

Meanwhile, Matanzas choked on the endless clatter of horse carriages and bicycles, the stench of manure so thick it crawled into throats and made people gag in the street, hands pressed to their mouths, eyes watering, children coughing into their mothers' skirts. Flies swarmed in black clouds, their buzz a maddening drone that followed every step, landing on bread, on open wounds, and on the sweat-slick faces of old men pushing carts loaded with nothing but hope. Police, their batons swinging at their sides, now patrolled even the fallen cyclists—a man with a broken leg, blood pooling dark on the asphalt, his cries ignored as officers blew whistles sharp as knives, herding the crowd forward like cattle. A woman knelt beside him, her voice cracking as she begged for help, but the patrol moved on, their boots thudding, leaving him to the heat and the flies. The important thing was animal traction, pushed full speed ahead, proving Cuba needed no gasoline—a hollow triumph of Castro's lunacy, hooves hammering over cracked pavement, over broken dreams, over the quiet, desperate tears of a city that had learned to breathe through the stink, to swallow the dust, to keep walking with empty stomachs and heavier hearts. A child clutched a crust of bread, its surface dotted with fly specks, her mother's hand trembling as she brushed the insects away, her "Eat, child" a whisper choked by the stench. An old man sat on the curb, his bare feet blistered from pushing a cart of wilted vegetables, his eyes fixed on the passing carriages, the horses' ribs stark beneath their hides, their breaths labored in the heat. A woman fainted in the street, her body crumpling to the asphalt, her neighbors lifting her with hands rough from work, their "Hold on" a plea lost in the clatter. The police watched, their batons still, their faces blank, their silence a weight heavier than the air. Liana stood at the corner, her heart a stone in her chest, Alina's hand warm in hers, her "Mommy, why do they cry?" a knife that cut deeper than the stink. The city moved, the hooves kept hammering, the dreams kept breaking, the tears kept falling—silent, endless, unstopped.

TIGHTENING SHADOWS

One day, a Cuban friend stopped Liana, Marko, and Alina on the street, his eyes darting, his voice low with fear, asking them never to visit again. The local Committees for the Defense of the Revolution had threatened him—foreigners at his home were beyond suspicious; the penalty would spill over his family and kids, a shadow of ruin. He asked them to walk to an alley. His back to the wall, his hands trembling as he lit a cigarette, the flame flickering in the humid air. "Don't come anymore," he whispered, his voice cracking, his eyes red from sleepless nights. Liana's heart sank; the warmth of their evenings together, the clink of plates, the laughter of children—all gone. Alina clutched her doll, her "Why?" a question that hung in the air, her small face pale. The friend knelt next to her, his "It's not safe," a whisper that broke Liana's heart, his hand on Alina's head a final touch. They walked away, the alley dark, the silence a weight, the friendship a memory that lingered in the dust. Liana's hands shook; the loss of their Cuban friend was a wound, the fear a chain that bound them. One after one, their circle of friends shrank, faces fading from their lives. People feared visiting them, their steps hesitant, and when

Liana and Marko went to their homes, they parked blocks away, their hearts pounding, but an eye always saw, watching from the dusk.

The discontent in the country continued, a low rumble in crowded markets. Some raised their voices in public, hunger, gasoline shortages, nonstop surveillance, and oppression, pushing them to risk everything, words sharp against the regime's weight. As disobedience grew, Castro's fist tightened brutally, no corner safe. Nowhere to hide—everyone was watched, no exceptions. At their complex's restaurant, an old man, tall, skin and bone, years heavy on his frame, adored Alina, her giggles a light in his weary eyes. She gave her heart back, always near him, sending kisses, clutching his hand, a reminder of her late grandpa. One day, returning from school, her red scarf flowing in the ocean breeze, he stepped out to greet her, both blowing kisses, waving hands, when the administrator—the "nazi," as kids called him—erupted, his military posture stark, barking threats to throw the man onto the street, a parasite in the regime's eyes. Seeing Liana on the balcony, his glare piercing, he snapped, "Get inside." Fear ruled, human dignity crushed, the pressure in Cuba's sealed vessel rising, ready to burst.

Hysteria surged, pathetic yet relentless. Liana thought it couldn't worsen, but Castro's speeches waved threats of Yankee invasion, his voice booming through crackling radios. Men and women left workplaces, donning green uniforms, with kids alone at home while parents defended against a phantom threat, rifles heavy in their hands. Why invade a self-disintegrating country? Its decay was its own ruin. Their compatriot friend in Havana, living with his Cuban family, was snatched by police—interrogated for 15 hours after visiting his in-laws in Miami, his voice hoarse from pleading. His home was torn apart: furniture splintered, television shattered, sons' beds ripped open, and toys scattered. They gave him 72 hours to leave with his wife and kids, a sentence barked without mercy. He didn't delay, abandoning everything, fleeing with only their lives. For two years, he fought to secure his wife's exit permit, each rejection a stab, hope fading in exile's shadow. While their lives were shattered, they were relieved to leave the island.

At school, the teacher gave the children a task: Write "Follow me," "We are happy here," "I am staying here," and "Yanki, faint this" dozens of times, slogans scrawled on tattered paper. Liana wished they had $3,000 in U.S. dollars for the international school to shield Alina from brainwashing, but paying in national pesos was impossible. "No, you're not writing this crap," Liana refused, anger flaring, earning another black mark for their family, a tally of defiance. When Alina asked about Romania's "martyr," Ceaușescu, eyes wide with confusion, Liana couldn't hold back—she told her he had the blood of innocents on his hands. Her true martyr was her grandpa, tortured by communists, his scars a silent testament. Quiet, perhaps for the first time, Alina leaned closer, wanting more. Then she asked why the man from the kitchen, a beloved friend, couldn't have bread, while the administrator's dog feasted on chicken, its bowl brimming with privilege. "We'll make sandwiches," Liana said, her voice low, "and sneak them to him, clandestinely." Liana realized how hard it was for her parents to shield her from negativity, her anger nearly spilling over, struggling to protect Alina from the world's weight.

Alina returned from school silent, with no wish to speak, shedding her uniform for shorts and a t-shirt, retreating to her room, the door creaking shut. Liana sensed her internal fight—the propaganda's relentless drumbeat clashing with their hushed truths. They couldn't speak openly; a child's slip could doom them. Even Liana struggled to sustain her anger, her fists clenched at the lies. How could she guide a child bombarded daily with communist slogans, their poison seeping into her young mind?

One evening, Liana's Cuban nurse friend and her doctor husband came to their home, both trembling, their voices agitated, the aluminum blinds clattering shut. The administration had warned them against foreign friends, nearly branding her a prostitute, a slur spat with venom. Liana was stunned, her blood boiling. The nurse—a decent woman, mother of two daughters, her hands still smelling of hospital antiseptic, her eyes always soft when she checked Alina's fever—stood in their kitchen, her uniform wrinkled, her wedding ring glinting under the dim bulb. "They said I was selling myself," she whispered, her voice cracking, tears spilling as her husband held her, his own face gray with rage and fear. Liana's heart shattered—this woman who had bandaged cuts, soothed nightmares, and shared rice from her own pot—reduced to filth by a word. They bravely visited a few more times, their steps cautious, parking blocks away, slipping through shadows, their daughters' drawings tucked in Alina's bag like secrets. But fear won. The visits stopped. The nurse vanished, her laughter gone, her warmth a memory. Years later, they escaped to America with their two young daughters, fleeing to freedom's uncertain shore, a whisper of hope carried on the wind, a family unbroken despite the shame, their courage a light Liana still carries.

Soon, Liana and Marko had no friends—the streets empty of familiar smiles, few daring to stop for fleeting chats, their words hurried under watchful eyes. The complex's children faced play restrictions, their laughter muted. One day, they adopted two orphaned puppies, tiny bundles of fur, eyes still sealed, whimpering in a cardboard box left by the gate. Alina named the runt Luz, her small hands cradling its shivering body, her "I'll keep you warm" a vow whispered in the dark. An Indian girl with braids claimed Leo, a bold golden pup who nipped her fingers with playful teeth. The kids gathered every dawn, their bare feet dusty, with old baby bottles clutched like treasures, milk dribbling down furry chins. They fought over who fed whom—the girl insisting Leo was hers, Alina guarding Luz like a lioness—their squeals a burst of joy that pierced the silence, and tails wagging furiously against cracked concrete. Liana watched, her heart swelling, the puppies' soft yelps a melody against the complex's gray walls. Sometimes the hugs were too tight, tiny ribs heaving under eager arms, and Liana gently pried them apart, her "Easy, loves" a soft command, her own eyes wet with the memory of Alina's first smile. The happiness was fleeting. One morning, the box was gone—vanished without a trace, the dirt still warm where it had sat. The children searched, frantic, their cries echoing off the buildings. Alina's "Where's Luz?" a sob that tore Liana's chest, the girl with braids screaming "Leo!" clutching her empty arms. They found only the administrator's stick-like figure, his boots planted, his face a mask of ice. Deaf to their pleas, blind to tears streaming down their faces, he savored the foreign children's pain, a slow, cruel relish. It was revolting. Amid Cuba's deficiencies, hunger gnawing, and lives fraying, why crush children's joy? Liana found no answer, no logic, only the hunger for control, a shadow over innocence. That night, Alina slept with her doll clutched tight, whispering "Luz … Leo …" into the dark, her small body shaking with dreams of lost warmth.

Every day, Liana fought to shield Alina from this suffocating world, her heart heavy with echoes of her own childhood, where her parents hid truths behind whispered tales, their voices soft in the dim light. Back in the Eastern European bloc, Liana had learned to smile through fear, a mask worn to survive, but now, watching Alina withdraw, her eyes dull with unspoken doubts, Liana feared the propaganda's grip. She remembered her father's scars, rough under her small fingers, and how he taught her to question, to hold fast to truth. Yet here, in Cuba's sealed cage, every word risked betrayal, and Liana struggled to balance honesty with safety, a tightrope over a void.

The regime's grip tightened further, its shadow creeping into every corner of their complex. New rules banned gatherings after dusk, even children's games were silenced, and the administrator prowled, his boots thudding on cracked pavement, logging every glance, every whisper. Neighbors turned inward, their doors locked tight, their warmth replaced by fear, a chill settling in the humid air. Once, they'd shared meals, plates clinking in cramped kitchens, but now, silence smothered them, the community fractured, each family an island. Liana felt the weight of their absence, a hollow ache, knowing the regime's surveillance had stolen not just friends but the very soul of their shared life.

Yet, in that darkness, a flicker of defiance burned. Late one night, the stars hidden by Matanzas' haze, Liana slipped a sandwich to the old man from the kitchen, the bread warm in her hands, Alina at her side, her slight nod a silent vow. They moved like shadows, their hearts racing, avoiding the administrator's gaze, his dog's distant bark a warning. It was a small act, a rebellion in whispers, but it lit a spark—a reminder of the humanity Cuba's regime couldn't crush, a hope Liana clung to for Alina, for them, as they faced the days ahead, braced for whatever came next.

The sandwich became a ritual, a secret born of love and fear. Every few nights, when the complex slept and the administrator's boots no longer echoed, Liana and Alina crept to the kitchen. The bread was stale, the cheese thin, but Liana wrapped it carefully, her fingers steady despite the tremor in her chest. Alina stood on a chair, her small hands pressing the napkin, her "For Grandpa" a whisper that filled the room. They slipped out the back door, the hinges squeaking softly, the humid air thick with the scent of salt and danger. The old man waited in the shadows, his tall frame bent, his eyes bright when he saw them. Alina ran to him, the sandwich warm in her hands, her "I made it" a gift that lit up his face. He took it with both hands, his "Thank you, little one" a voice cracked with age and hunger, his kiss on her forehead a blessing. Liana watched, her heart full, the administrator's dog still a distant bark, the surveillance a weight she pushed away. The tradition grew. The sandwiches changed—sometimes with a slice of tomato, sometimes just bread and salt—but the love was constant. Alina drew pictures on the napkin, her "For you" a heart that made the old man tear up. Liana added notes, her "You are not alone," a whisper that carried them through the dark. The risk was real—the administrator's eyes, the dog's bark, and the neighbors' silence—but the love was stronger. The old man's stories came, his voice low, his tales of the sea a light in the gray. Alina listened, her head on his knee, her "Tell me more" a plea that mended Liana's heart. The sandwiches were a rebellion, the love a fire, the hope a spark that burned in the dark.

ONE FAITHFUL DAY

One day, Alina returned from school, her face tragically pale, her breathing heavy, her eyes wide with panic. From their apartment's windows, Liana saw a massive cloud, thick and menacing, swiftly enveloping their building, its acrid haze seeping through cracks. Liana shoved a blanket under the door, coughing, gasping for air alongside Alina, their lungs stinging. Wetting two towels, their damp weight a frail shield, Liana pressed them to their faces, protecting them from the poison streaming through closed blinds. For hours, they fought for breath, their eyes red, tears streaming, their throats burning from the toxic substance, their breaths fast and shallow. Rayonera and Cubanitro spewed their byproducts unchecked, poisoning Matanzas once again, with no controls in sight. Nearby stood the maternity and municipal hospitals, a specialty clinic, and schools, all choked by the same fumes. Liana wondered if studies existed on the city's respiratory illnesses—their medical friends whispered of child mortality soaring, a truth silenced, its weight crushing parents' hopes.

The cloud hung like a shroud, the air thick with the chemical bite, the windows rattling with the wind. Liana held Alina close, her small body trembling, her "Mommy, it hurts" a sob that tore Liana's heart. The towels grew damp with tears and breath, the poison seeping through, the room a tomb. Liana's chest burned, her coughs racking, her "Breathe, baby" a whisper that hung in the air. The hours stretched, the cloud a weight, the silence a chain. The hospitals choked, the schools were silent, and the children were coughing in the dust. Liana's resolve hardened; the poison was fire, the truth a spark that burned in her heart.

Liana decided to document these atrocities against young and old; no effort was made to curb the industrial poison. Daily, she took pictures from their apartment or near the plants, coughing, vomiting, suffocated by the chemical stench, its bite lingering in her throat. She photographed openly, never thinking to hide it, until one day a maintenance person stopped her, his voice low and urgent, "Let's go behind the building to talk." Her heart pounding, Liana followed. "Don't talk at home—they have listening devices, even in our office," he said, his voice trembling, glancing around. "You've attracted the authorities' attention—you're under surveillance. Don't talk on the phone, at home, anywhere," his warning as sharp as a blade. He pointed to a green Moskvich, a Soviet relic with "Empresa Eléctrica" signs, parked ominously. Fear coiled in Liana's gut as he hurried back, his footsteps fading into the dark.

Shock gave way to dread—could it be true? What had Liana done? Only photographed the white clouds billowing from the chemical plants, their poison cloaking the city? Her naivety was shattered. Days later, Liana noticed men in the adjacent building, never arriving or leaving together, one always inside, with large microphones glinting behind half-closed blinds, aimed at them. The gap was mere feet, close enough to catch their every word, a net of surveillance tightening. It felt unreal, like a movie where they were the prey, their lives the main act, played out under unseen eyes. Liana alerted Marko, her voice urgent, but he laughed, dismissing her. "Talk to the maintenance person, look through the windows," she pleaded—nothing swayed him. Women's fears, too often brushed off as "emotional," stung, but Liana would soon prove her truth, at a cost too close to death.

The men were shadows, their faces blank, their microphones a menace in the dark. Liana watched from the window, her heart pounding, the blinds a barrier that wasn't. The men in guayaberas came, the white fabric crisp, their briefcases heavy. The surveillance was a weight, the fear a chain. The complex was a cage, the neighbors silent, the love a memory.

A month before July 26, a second apartment filled with white guayaberas. The blinds there were always shut tight, people coming and going, the complex's "nazi" often there. One day, making herself look as innocent as possible, Liana asked one of them, as he tucked his guayabera and black briefcase into the car, if he was a doctor and who was sick here. "I am a doctor of social illnesses," was his response, and Liana thought, "Cynic." At that time, the food situation in the country was dire; the coupon books now lasted two years, the rice quotas slashed. Every person who escaped the country meant one less quota; soon, the regime would ask citizens to deny their own lives, but the spying would never cease.

Filled with rage at the endless poison choking Matanzas, Liana kept taking pictures—now hiding her film. She and Alina fled to Mexico City, their lungs straining in the thin air, their hearts lifting at the Wax Museum's lifelike figures, the National Palace's grandeur, and Teotihuacan's warm ancient stones under their hands. For the first time, no police, no shadows—just strangers smiling, calling them "gringas," a lightness they'd forgotten. Clutching the developed photos—a small packet of truth—they returned, with hearts lifted yet wary, the spark of hope burning against the weight of what awaited.

July 26 neared, Fidel Castro's visit turning Matanzas into a fortress, buzzing with the roar of helicopters, cars, navy ships in the gulf, jets screaming overhead, snipers perched, their rifles glinting. Cannons pointed skyward, a city braced for war. The morning before his arrival, Liana walked the complex, breezy warmth mocking the tension confined within the fence, the eyes of snipers tracking every move. Near the fence's edge, a tall man in a guayabera, face serious, approached, claiming he was visiting them, his tone too smooth. Thinking him Marko's colleague, Liana let him in, but for five hours, he probed with a million questions, his surprising knowledge of their lives chilling. Liana spotted a gun bulging under his guayabera, her pulse racing, whispering to Marko, "I don't trust him—something's wrong." As a helicopter roared above, carrying Fidel Castro back to Havana, its shadow darkening the room, he stood, saying in their language, almost with no accent, "My work here is done," and left, footsteps echoing like a threat.

Liana's heart froze—he knew everything they'd exchanged, every word a trap. It wasn't a joke—they were under close watch, their family branded enemies of the revolution, danger encircling them all. The regime spared no expense, mountains of effort to crush threats, their gaze unyielding. Days later, Liana noticed items in their apartment misplaced, books shifted, papers askew. Small tests confirmed her fears—intruders had come, silent as shadows. Her pictures vanished, stolen in haste, but the negatives, hidden deep, escaped their grasp. She hid her notebooks with a trusted friend, fearing they would vanish like her stolen photographs.

The men next door kept spying, blinds half-open, while Liana played blind, her heart pounding with every glance. Branded as threats, their family marked, Liana didn't waver—aggressively working on her plan to obtain a visa to visit Miami, inspired by its radio's lifeline. It was a desperate bid for freedom that became the regime's last straw, sparking their resolve to eliminate her family. Liana and Marko planned to travel to the U.S. Interests Section in Havana, operated under the protection of the Swiss Embassy. Filled with almost effervescent enthusiasm, Liana couldn't wait to wake that morning, donning her best clothes, packing sandwiches and water bottles, and calling Alina to hurry. Alina begged to stay, playing with the complex's kids, her laughter a rare spark of joy. Liana hesitated—what could happen?—leaving her behind, trusting she'd be safe.

Marko drove, coffee warm in their hands, music humming, the road stretching free. Liana envisioned walking into the U.S. Interests Section, getting her visa, traveling with the pictures of Cubanitro and Rayonera's poisonous clouds enveloping the city, and sharing them with the radio stations that sustained her hope for change. It wasn't meant to be. Throughout the entire time, a Lada trailed them, its engine growling, matching their speed and slowing when they did. It was not meant to be to get the visa—Liana was told she had to return to her country and apply from there. Disappointment choked her to tears, her heart broken inside.

On their drive back home, as they entered the mountainous part of the road, the Lada still trailing them, its exhaust fumes bitter in the air, Liana saw a second car approaching, its tires humming on asphalt. As they climbed a hill, the sun glaring off the windshield, Liana turned and saw that the man sitting next to the driver of the closest car had a gun, its barrel aimed at them, the man staring with cold, unyielding eyes. Liana got scared and told Marko; he pressed the gas, the engine roaring, and as they passed Punta Jibacoa, both cars surged closer, their metal frames gleaming under the Cuban sun, tires screeching against the asphalt, trying to force them off a cliff where the earth dropped hundreds of feet to the crashing waves below.

The first impact came suddenly—metal on metal, the Skoda lurching. "They're pushing us!" Liana screamed, her hands clawing the empty seat where Alina should have been, the child's absence a hollow ache. Marko swerved, tires screaming, the cliff rushing closer, rocks tumbling into the void. The second Lada roared up alongside, sandwiching them, engines snarling, the gunman's face a mask behind the windshield. Liana's world narrowed to the edge—the sea a hungry mouth, the drop certain death. Alina's face flashed in her mind, her laughter at the complex, her "Mommy, come back soon," a plea that tore Liana's soul. "Not her, not like this," she sobbed, her body bracing for the fall. Marko floored it, the engine howling in protest, the car tilting, one wheel skimming the brink, with gravel raining into the abyss. Time slowed—the wind howling, the sea roaring—Alina's forgotten doll on the dashboard staring with button eyes.

A Havanatur bus lumbered into view, its horn a thunderclap. Marko braked hard; the Skoda skidded, smoke pouring from the tires. The Ladas shot past, mission failed. The bus stopped, tourists gaping, with drivers rushing to help.

Liana collapsed against Marko, her body shaking, tears hot on her cheeks, the cliff's edge a scar in her mind. "Alina," she whispered —the name a prayer, survival a miracle under the Cuban sun. Marko's hands trembling, he raced them home, the road blurring through tears. At the complex, Liana saw Alina playing, safe with friends, and ran to her, hugging her close, thanking God for her life, for theirs. Terrifying fear gnawed at Liana's bones. Invisible forces, hostile and uncompromising, decided their fate, their dogmas inhuman, nothing sacred to a regime that branded dissenters as enemies. They'd escaped death, but the threat loomed, its eyes locked on theirs.

The next day, still shaking from the fear they had experienced, Liana walked to the beach. Outside the fence of the complex, she saw a young man, so poor it struck her—his clothes in rags, his shoes falling apart, and a hat screaming a hundred years old. As Liana passed him, she turned again; he provoked such pity. Then she saw him take a little radio from his pocket, talking to someone. Liana thought that this was a country where half of Cuba spies on the other half; they have no money for food, but their military apparatus and State Security are fully funded and licensed to surveil and kill. Why were they still here?

One path remained—return home, where danger might fade, forgotten in time. Liana looked at Alina—this wasn't her life, no reason justified a Damocles' sword over them, least of all without parents. Staying in Cuba another day was a crime, Liana's heart refusing a regime's destiny. She issued an ultimatum—they must leave, now, her resolve ironclad, no longer swayed by love for Cuba's people, their warmth a fading echo. Little did Liana know she'd face a similar choice later, back home. That day, she realized the regime knew her plans—films, Mexico, Miami. They spoke via notes, even as they taught Alina, their pens scratching in silence. Marko's botched hernia surgery left him in pain, the jagged scar a testament to socialist medicine's failure. Liana lived in a haze, suspicious of every shadow, fear a constant pulse. Alina's life made leaving nonnegotiable; the only way. This time, no one pushed Liana onto the plane—she didn't cry, didn't look back, happy to leave Cuba, forever, ready to face the uncertain path ahead.

TO LEAVE YOUR COUNTRY BEHIND

Returning home was bittersweet—Liana's father's absence loomed over them, her mother's hope that they never leave her alone, friends who missed them, and some who had forgotten them. The hope for freedom burned stronger than ever; Liana and Marko knew the only path was to seek it. Still, fear gnawed at them. Would their diplomas be accepted in America? Would authorities there jail them? From a young age, they were bombarded with disinformation. Propaganda was a relentless drumbeat—posters screaming from every corner, teachers droning, radio crackling lies, static buzzing in their ears. It worked. Liana swallowed chunks of that poison, bitter in her throat, despite the defiance she nursed in secret. If people think brainwashing can't pierce the toughest mind, think again. Escape beyond the Iron Curtain? They were told for years it was a fool's dream—only arrest, prison, a slow rot in some Western cell awaited dissidents.

Deciding to leave was a blade through Liana's heart. No matter the hardships, the desperation, family and country are a bond hard to break. After her homeland and Cuba failed them, their promises dust in Liana's mouth, and accepting reality hurt. But a country isn't just dirt and borders—it's roots, blood, kin's voices echoing in every corner. Walking away shook Liana loose, her gravity gone, no anchor, with despair and hope boiling inside. Her city's streets, the bakery's warm yeast scent, her mother's voice over tea, memories of her father's quiet pride, and friends she might never see again. That road stretched brutally, especially through Cuba, each step a fight between fear and faith.

Marko escaped first, slipping through the regime's grasp. Soon after, Liana realized a communist regime doesn't forget those who keep their heads up, doesn't forgive defiance—it strikes back, punishing with force, no regret. When she learned her "missteps" trailed her from Cuba, whispers of rebellion hissing, Alina's future used as a bargaining chip to make Liana bow her head "lower than grass," dread turned icy in her veins. The threat rang in her ears: obedience or lose Alina to slavery in the Middle East. Liana had no choice but to choose freedom. She organized friends to pick Alina up from school when she was late from work. She didn't leave her daughter alone for a second. Selling the beautiful old Bechstein piano that her aunts left her provided the money to finance the next steps. Liana found a company that sent young children to America as exchange students. The requirement was English language fluency. In three months, Alina studied to pass the test, and Liana finally sent her to safety—her absence a hollow ache. Months passed without seeing her. Alina's calls from America didn't go through—always something with satellites—her letters never arriving. But one day, she reached Liana, her voice different, her conviction and resolve shining as never before. "Mom, I will never leave America," she said, loud and clear, hitting Liana's heart like a knife, spurring her to desperately seek a way to reach free land, to be with her family, America a distant beacon pulling her forward.

Leaving the country was no easy task. Liana needed a new passport—nearly impossible for a known rebel. Desperate, her hope fading, a miracle unfolded—she believed God had His ways to guide lives, to breathe new life, to open paths unseen. One day, unexpectedly, she met a man with a strong hand and soft heart, truly God-sent. He helped her get a passport and escorted her to the plane to a neutral third country where she hoped to apply for a U.S. visa. Once there, Liana slept on hard floors, city clamor ringing in her ears, roaming penniless for over a month. It wasn't meant to be—she received the same answer as in Havana—and then she escaped.

The road was no bed of roses. In that third country, Liana caught an infection that brought her near sepsis, fever searing her bones, her body shuddering, desperate that she'd die before seeing Alina again. God had other plans, nursing her back with a gentle hand, her heart swelling with gratitude, her hope rekindled like a flame in her chest. Then Liana finally realized she was free—at home in America, Alina beside her, breathing new strength into her weakened body, shining light in her life, making all sacrifices insignificant compared to the happiness of having her close.

Liana stepped onto American soil, a stranger with a battered suitcase, the Miami sun searing her skin—its heat a kinder fire than Cuba's relentless dust. The air pulsed with chaos—cars honking, voices clashing in Spanish and English, a city alive with the rhythm of freedom. Alina, now a teenager, stood beside her, blonde hair catching the light, her eyes wide with a resolve that echoed Liana's own. The weight of their escape—the Lada's snarl, the cliff's jagged maw, the hidden negatives of Matanzas' toxic clouds—lingered like a bruise. But here, under an open sky, Liana felt her spine straighten, her breath deepen. America was no utopia, its streets rough with struggle, but its promise lay in the absence of Party shadows, the chance to build without unseen eyes.

Their first apartment was a shoebox, its walls thin as their old Cuban shack, but the hum of a refrigerator—stocked with milk and fruit—felt like a miracle. Liana found work cleaning houses, her hands raw from bleach, the scent a sharp reminder of the hospitals in Matanzas. Yet each dollar earned was hers, not rationed by a regime. Alina enrolled in school, her Spanish slang fading into English, her laughter unbound as she joined a debate club, her voice sharp with arguments Liana had once whispered in secret. Nights, they sat on a sagging couch, sharing stories of Guantánamo's dusty streets, the doctor's gentle hands, and the children's hugs—their warmth a tether to a past they couldn't erase. Liana taught Alina to cook her mother's recipes—potatoes roasted crisp, cake baked for birthdays—each bite a rebellion against the hunger they'd known. Alina's eyes, once shadowed by the weight of propaganda, sparkled with dreams of becoming a journalist; her resolve to fight for others was a spark kindled in Cuba's dust.

The adjustment wasn't seamless. Liana woke to nightmares of sirens, her heart racing at the memory of boots thudding, guayaberas lurking. The shadow of PTSD never left her. The city's noise—car horns, streets packed with people—jarred her, a reminder of Havana's chaos, but here, no one demanded her silence. She called her mother daily, the phone's crackle a lifeline across oceans, her voice a balm to the ache of absence. When savings grew, she flew her mother to Miami—her arrival a burst of light. Christmas became their ritual: the tree adorned with Alina's paper ornaments, a nod to Guantánamo's defiance, her mother's laughter mingling with Alina's as they strung lights under the humid Florida sky. Those months, filled with stories of Liana's father—his war tales, his ninety-nine bears—were a tapestry of memory, weaving their past into this new land.

But freedom carried new chains. Liana watched Alina navigate America's chaos—school cliques, the pressure to fit in—and feared the digital age's creeping control, screens demanding loyalty as fiercely as Party slogans. Her old regime would've envied this—thoughts exposed, no whispers needed. Liana taught Alina to question, to guard her truth, just as her father had taught her, his scars a lesson in resilience. When her mother fell ill, American doctors saved her—a stark contrast to Cuba's empty wards—but her death years later left a wound that bled daily, a scar beside the engineer's loss, the Cuban children's hugs. Yet Alina's laughter, her fierce pursuit of justice, anchored Liana. She built a life—brick by brick, a house free of surveillance, a new job, her voice steady as she shared truths no regime could silence. America's open skies, its grit and promise, were worth every fight—a beacon Liana vowed to protect for Alina, for all who'd bled for freedom.

Marko and Liana drifted further apart—years on separate continents, stress crushing them, tragedies carving silence between them. They grieved differently, the loss of a friend a wound that never closed. Marko couldn't assimilate, never felt at home in the U.S., his heart tethered to Cuba's warmth, where he was happiest. Until his last day, he was surrounded by his faithful Cuban friends.

Embracing the United States, pain still lingered—tears for what Liana had left, worries about the future—but hope and strong will won. On a new soil, every day, Liana gave thanks to God, guided by His hand. Day after day, she felt more American than ever—loving this land's chaos, its promise, profoundly grateful for doors flung wide, a chance she'd never dreamed of.

Years later, one sleepless night, terrified by the divide in the country, worried about the future, Liana took out her notebooks—pages yellowed from years in a cabinet, waiting to come alive. Her writing, uneven and sometimes hard to read, was proof of the extreme emotional stress she'd lived under. She looked at photos of her daughter and grandchildren and realized she had only one path ahead of her.

She sat at her desk, the laptop emitting an inviting light in the darkened room. She opened a new Word document and wrote:

"The Cuban Manuscript"
by Liana S.

www.ingramcontent.com/pod-product-compliance
Lightning Source LLC
LaVergne TN
LVHW090612110826
845146LV00001B/350